MW00987005

DEATH ON BAINBRIDGE ISLAND

Pacific Northwest Cozy Culinary Mystery Series - Book 3

Dennis Shock

Copyright © 2023 by Dennis Shock

All rights reserved.

No portion of this book may be reproduced in any form without written permission from the publisher or author, except as permitted by U.S. copyright law.

1

Brick sat at attention, looking out the window as rain streamed down the glass pane. The apricot, curly-haired Goldendoodle was fixated on Judy walking towards her mother's condo with something tucked under her raincoat. As the knob on the front door turned, Nellie started to bark, while staying a good ten feet from the door. Brick moved to the edge of the entrance and stood in anticipation of the visitor. His body wagged with eagerness. The short, stout PBGV stopped her bark and copied Brick's body wag as Judy entered. Judy crossed the threshold, pulling a small black and tan Yorkshire Terrier from under her pastel blue raincoat. She knelt, letting the other dogs sniff the small dog. "This is Jack," Judy said to the two larger dogs. "He's our new family member. You two be nice to Jack." Jack's eyes widened for a few seconds, but after some initial sniffing, the dogs all seemed to relax, and Judy placed the puppy on the floor. There was running, jumping, and quite a bit of barking, mostly by the puppy. Nellie seemed cautiously interested, and Brick refused to get into full play mode. That was probably for the best since the fifty-pound, curly-haired dog towered over the two-pound pup.

"Oh, good. You finally brought Jack over for a visit," Lily said as she came from the back of the home. "I know you were worried about Nellie since she's a little sensitive, but Brick is very well-mannered around other dogs and may help them work things out. I'm sure they will all get along just fine."

"How long is Brick staying with you," Judy asked as she shed her raincoat, leaving it on the doorknob to drip on the tile entry.

"Just a couple of days. Jed is at a food expo. He should be back late tomorrow. He's very loveable and well-mannered." Lily smiled at the large dog.

"Are you talking about Brick or Jed," Judy said with a laugh.

"True of both, I guess, but I was referring to the dog."

"Why do you look like you're dressed for work?"

"I have to go to the restaurant. I'm sorry. I know we planned to spend the morning together, but Chase didn't show up for work this morning. Linda just called a few minutes ago. I need to help them get opened, and I'll stay through lunch if he doesn't show up."

"I'll hang out here with the dogs in case you can come back. They could use the chance to get to know one another. I have some work to do. I'll grab my laptop from the car."

"What are you working on?"

"Ferry boat scheduling changes are on the horizon. Big story," she chuckled. "I have a piece on travel to Canada due after that. I think I have a new angle on it. I'm working on both stories right now. I should have the scheduling piece finished pretty quickly. What's the story with Chase? He's usually pretty reliable, isn't he?"

"Yes. Very."

Chase Raker was the front-of-house manager at Lily's restaurant along Liberty Bay in Poulsbo. He had been with her since she opened last year. Lily relied on him and Linda Holt to hold everything together at the restaurant when she wasn't there, and sometimes when she was.

"Doesn't he date that nice girl over at Virgil's café?" Judy asked.

"Yes. Her name is Annie Beazley. I'll check with her to see if she's heard from him. Good idea. The wonderful mind of an investigative reporter," Lily said with a chortle.

"I'll grab my laptop quickly before you leave. Keep an eye on Jack."

"Will do. He sure is an adorable little guy."

"He certainly is. Just like you two," Judy said as she scratched the chins of the other two dogs.

Lily's phone rang as Judy left the condo. She accepted a call from the Bainbridge Island Sherriff's Department and spoke briefly to someone on the other end. She hung up the phone call as Judy reentered her home.

"What's wrong, Mom?" Judy asked. "You have an unsettled look on your face."

"I just talked to Chase. He's in lockup at the Bainbridge Police Station. He's not sure when he'll be able to get out."

"What's the charge?"

"Murder."

2

"I 'll get on the phone and the internet. If I can find out who's been appointed council, maybe we can get in to see him." Judy opened her laptop and started tapping away.

"I'm going to go down to Virgil's Café to talk to Annie. Then, I'll go on to work. I'm not clear why he called me instead of calling her. I'm stunned by the entire conversation. He said his roommate is dead and that the police have reason to believe he is responsible. He said he didn't know who else to call. He ended the call by saying, 'Please help me.'"

"If I can get ahold of someone to find out if we can talk with him, I'll come pick you up. We should get over there to see if we can help him. Did he tell you he didn't do it?"

"He didn't say either way. I assume he's innocent. I can't imagine Chase being responsible for someone else's death unless it was some sort of terrible accident. After I talk to Annie, I'll help Linda with a lunch plan. Hopefully, by then, you'll have news about what we can do to help."

Lily grabbed her raincoat and hurried to her SUV. The drive was short, but she didn't want to walk it in the rain. She parked along the street between her restaurant and Virgil's. Lily pushed the dripping hood from her head as the bell on the café door rang. She came face to face with Annie at the entrance.

"Grab a seat anywhere, Lily. I'll be right with you." Annie dropped the coffee pot she was holding onto the counter and turned towards the window between the grill and the dining room. Virgil slid plates of steaming food into the window.

Annie reached for two of the full breakfast plates. As she turned around, Lily grabbed her tenderly by the shoulder. "Annie. I got a call from the Bainbridge Island Police Station. Chase has been arrested."

Annie stared blankly at Lily for a moment and then a tear rolled down her cheek. "Arrested? Why was he arrested?" She asked softly at a volume barely audible over the noise coming from the kitchen.

"He said his roommate died. I don't know much more than that. Judy is trying to dig up further information. We hope to get the chance to speak with him. I can let you know the minute we have some details."

"I would appreciate that. Is there anything I can do for Chase right now? Anything I can do to help him?" Annie asked as she pulled in a quivering breath. The bell at the front door jingled behind them.

"I don't think there is anything you can do at the moment. I'm going to Marty's to help Linda prepare for lunch. I'll call you the minute we know more."

"Thank you. I should get these breakfast plates out. I'll be watching for your call. I'll stay here for now if there isn't anything else I can do. I can try to get someone to come in here to cover for me so that I can go to Bainbridge Island once we can see him."

"Do you want me to talk to Virgil for you?" Lily offered, looking through the pass-through window at the old man working away at the grill.

"No. That's okay. I'll do that. He'll understand." Annie patted Lily's hand, which still rested on her shoulder, and turned away to grab the two breakfast plates she had set down while they talked. Annie carried the plates to a table near the back of the restaurant. She took out her order pad as she moved to another table where three men had seated themselves while Annie and Lily had been talking. Lily shook her head in bewilderment as she turned to leave the café.

3

— . —

"**M**om, Piper Baxter is Chase's court-appointed attorney. She can get us in to see him. Ready to go?" Judy asked as she appeared in the restaurant office.

"Yes. I think Linda and David have this all under control. Let's go see if we can help Chase. I'll call Annie to see if she wants to come with us." Lily poked her thumb at her cell phone screen and put the phone to her ear. The two women left the restaurant. The call went to voice mail as the double-parked Jeep Wrangler left the alley behind Marty's on the Bay.

"She didn't answer?" Judy asked.

"No. That's strange. I can't believe she wasn't waiting for my call."

"I'll pull up in front of Virgil's Café, and you can run in."

Lily nodded and redialed her phone. The call went to voice mail again. The Jeep came to a stop, and Lily jumped out to run through the downpour. She was only inside for a minute.

"She wasn't in there. Virgil said she called Tonia to cover for her and ran out the door the minute Tonia showed up. He has no idea where she went."

"Maybe she went to Bainbridge on her own. I couldn't blame her. She's probably worried sick about her boyfriend. I'm sure she isn't thinking straight. It's surprising that she didn't take off the minute you told her about his call."

"I found her initial reaction to be a bit odd, but then, I don't know how I should have expected her to react. This situation has never come up for me before."

"Oh, really? Come on. Are you trying to tell me this is the first time you've gotten a call from a man who's been arrested for murder? I assumed that happened to you at least once a week."

"Not a good time for sarcasm."

"Just trying to lighten the mood."

"Did the court-appointed attorney give you any information about what happened?"

"Chase's roommate, Ron Castle, was found dead on the couch of their apartment early this morning. Neighbors reported Chase screaming at Ron around three in the morning. The police found Chase passed out along the road outside of town."

"David said he and Chase were drinking over in Seattle last night. They took the 2:10 ferry back to the island and split up when they left the terminal. Neither of them lives very far from the pier."

"Is Chase an angry drunk? Maybe he did kill Ron?"

"'I've' never heard anything about him getting mean or belligerent when he drinks. I have heard a few stories from David, Annie, and Chase about their drinking habits. They are all known to tie one on. Most of Chase's stories start with 'We had had a few too many...' but the stories always end in an amusing way not a tragic turn of events."

"Maybe this was the exception. He wouldn't be the first person to lose control in a drunken stupor and hurt someone. I guess we'll find out soon enough," Judy commented as the bright red SUV bounced onto the Agate Passage Bridge.

4

Piper, Judy, and Lily sat facing Chase on one side of a large metal table. Chase wore a pair of faded jeans and a wrinkled polo. His hair stood up on one side, and his eyes were beet red. He stared blankly at the table between them.

"Chase, are you okay?" Lily asked.

"Can you tell us what happened?" Piper added.

Chase sat silently for several minutes. The ladies waited quietly until Judy couldn't bare it any longer. "We can't help you if you don't talk to us. Tell us what you know."

Chase rubbed the stubble on his face with the back of his hand without making eye contact with any of the women who sat across from him. "I don't know what happened. I went out drinking last night. I came back on the late ferry and walked home."

"Witnesses reported hearing you yell at Ron. It seems the apartment walls are pretty thin, and you were very loud," Piper said when Chase paused to take a deep breath.

"I did yell at him. I was mad, but I didn't kill him. I didn't do anything to him." Chase looked up for the first time. He looked into Lily's eyes. "I didn't hurt him. I never touched him. Honest."

"I believe you," Lily said as her eyes met his. She felt bad for the young man. She had known him for only about a year, but she couldn't imagine this gentle soul doing anything to harm another human being.

"You need to tell us what you remember. You have to give us something to go on if you want us to believe you." Judy wasn't as convinced of his innocence.

"She's right, Chase. We need to start working on your defense," Piper chimed in. "You're going to be sent to Kitsap County Corrections in Port Orchard. There are some rough characters in there. The sooner we can get to the bottom of this, the better. I know the DA on this one. He wouldn't have charged you if he didn't think he had a case. Tell us what you remember. If anyone else was with you or saw you last night, that would be helpful."

Chase took another long breath and started to speak, "David and I had been drinking in Seattle. We had a few too many, as usual, and barely made the 2:10 ferry to the island. We parted ways at the terminal, and I went home. Ron was laying on the couch when I walked in. The apartment was a mess. I was drunk and upset about the state of the kitchen and family room. I started yelling at him about it. I'm sure that's what the neighbors heard. I stormed out and that was the last I saw of him. I have no idea when or how he died. I wasn't in the apartment for long."

"The preliminary report from the coroner puts his time of death between two and five in the morning. Are you saying he was alive and well when you left him?" Piper was clarifying. "The ferry would have gotten in around two forty. Depending on your walking speed, you likely couldn't have made it home much before three."

"What did he say to you?" Judy asked. "Did he argue with you about the apartment? Was there any type of physical confrontation? Did you strike him or assault him in any way?"

"No!" Chase exclaimed. His jaw started to quiver as he spoke. "We didn't argue. We didn't fight. He just laid there on the sofa. He ignored me completely. That's why I stormed out. His apathy made me even madder."

"Did he move at all? Did he react to you in any way?" Lily asked.

"No. He laid in front of the TV without even turning his head... ignoring me." Chase's words grew softer.

"Lily looked at the other two women and then back to Chase. "Is there any chance that he was already dead when you got home? Are you sure he was alive when you were in the apartment yelling at him?"

Chase squinted his eyes and rubbed them sternly. He blinked a few times as if he could see the past in front of him. His eyes dropped to the table between them as if he were in a deep trance. His breath grew heavy. It was the only sound in the room for several seconds. He started to shake his head slowly and methodically. "I don't know. It's all so hazy. I was drunk, mad, and tired. It's not unusual for him to ignore me when he's watching TV. That's why I started yelling. I wanted to make him listen."

"You can't say for sure if he moved at all while you were there. Is that what you are saying?" Piper was interested in Lily's line of thinking.

"I'm just not sure. I mean… I thought he was lying on the couch watching TV like he always does. He stays up late watching movies all the time. I hadn't considered that anything was wrong with him at the time." Chase rested his elbows on the table and let his face drop into his hands.

"If we can somehow prove that Ron died before you got home, you'll be in the clear. This could be a very big break," Piper said. "I wish public defenders had their own investigators assigned. We need to find out about Ron's day leading up to the murder. According to the coroner's report, Ron died of blunt-force trauma. He was apparently struck with a fairly large object at the top of his head. Anyone could have struck him from that angle while he was in a reclining position on the sofa. No sign of a break-in. It seems like it was likely someone Ron knew."

"How did the police find the body? Did someone report it?" Judy asked, looking up from a small notepad she was using to keep track of the conversation.

"One of the neighbors reported a noise disturbance. Likely Chase's shouting. When the police arrived, the door was ajar, and there was no answer. They entered to find Ron Castle dead." Piper read from a report she had pulled from her briefcase.

"What time was that?" Lily asked, glancing down at the report in front of Piper.

"Five fourteen," Piper responded.

"Chase, do you know if you closed the door on your way out?" Judy asked.

"I have no idea. I'm sure I didn't bother to lock it. In the state I was in, I can't say for sure if I closed it or not. Do you think I left the door open for someone to walk in and kill Ron?" Tears started to roll down his face as he looked to the lawyer for answers.

"It's very hard to say what happened at this time. We need to gather as much information as we can and raise doubt in the case against you. That is our main focus. My job is to get you off the hook for murder. First and foremost, we need to find a way to prove you didn't kill Ron," Piper replied in a confident manner.

"We will help with the investigation on your behalf," Judy stated as she studied Chase's expression. "I'm an investigative reporter. It's what I do. I'll get over to your apartment building and find out what I can from the neighbors. Is there anything else you can tell us? Did you talk to anyone besides Ron at your apartment complex this morning? Is there anyone that can substantiate your timeline?"

"I don't remember seeing anyone else. It was the middle of the night," he said.

"When were you last in the apartment before coming back from Seattle?" Lily asked.

"Early yesterday, before work. I left home around seven. David and I went to Bremerton with Annie after work, and then, David and I took the Bremerton ferry to Seattle. We ate dinner at Pikes Market and then hit some bars," Chase said.

"Do you have any idea what Ron was doing during the time you and David were in Seattle? Where he was? Who he was with?" Judy asked.

"I don't," Chase said. "Ron and I shared rent but that was about it. We didn't get along very well. I spend very little time at the apartment. I sleep there part of the time. I shower and do my laundry there. Otherwise, I'm at work, at Annie's, or out with friends. Yesterday was Ron's day off. He's a bit of a homebody. Judging by the food remains that covered the kitchen and living room, I'd guess he spent most of the day at home. From the number of beer bottles and to-go containers laying around, I assumed he had some company. Likely Sam and Juice. They are always hanging around the apartment."

"Do Sam and Juice have last names?" Piper questioned Chase.

"Sam Castle and Julius Barbor. Sam is Ron's little brother. Julius is Sam's friend. Everyone calls him Juice," Chase responded.

"The police have likely already canvassed the apartment complex. Maybe you can get the neighbors to share their stories with you as well." Piper looked at Judy. "I have the name of the neighbor who filed the complaint."

Piper turned the file towards Judy and tapped on a line near the middle of one of the reports. Judy nodded and quickly scribbled some notes on her pad.

"We'll figure all of this out, Chase," Lily stated confidently.

"Thank you both," Chase said as Lily and Judy moved towards the door.

"Let's go over everything one more time. I want to lock down the timeline." Piper remained seated across from Chase.

5

—·—

"What do you think, Mom?" Judy had started the Jeep but left it in park, looking at her mother.

"About what?" Lily looked quizzically at her daughter.

"Do you think he did it?"

"Killed his roommate? Not for a minute. Chase would never do something like that. I don't care how drunk he was."

"It could have been an accident. Maybe he threw something at him in a fit of rage or pushed him down."

"I think he would have come clean. He would have called an ambulance. He's a kind and caring person. He's an honest person. When he first started working for me, he left an entire case of steaks out of the cooler overnight. He could have cast the blame elsewhere, but he owned up to it right away. He counts down the cash at night at the restaurant. I've never had so much as a penny come up missing. I find it hard to believe he's lying to us."

"Murder is a compelling reason to lie. This isn't like losing your job stuff. This is life in prison stuff."

"You could be right, but I have a good feeling about him. I believe he's innocent. We need to help him."

"Okay then. Let's see what we can do about proving you're right." Judy put the Wrangler in drive and directed the vehicle toward Chase's apartment complex. She had noted his address from the file Piper shared with her.

Minutes later they were knocking on Elenore Petrovsky's door. Elenore lived to one side of Ron and Chase in apartment 206. She was the neighbor who had called in the disturbance on the night in question.

They waited in the hallway for several minutes after knocking. No one answered. "I imagine Miss Petrovsky is at work. We will have to come back this evening," Judy said. She pulled a napkin from her pocket and covered the doorknob to apartment 204 with it, trying to turn the covered knob."

"There's crime tape across the door. You can't go in there." Lily tried to stop her daughter's motion.

"If it was unlocked, I wanted to take a quick look. It was worth a try. Let's check with the neighbor on the other side." Judy moved to the door labeled 202 and started knocking once more.

They heard movement inside and were quickly greeted by a tall man with a high forehead and long black hair. He looked down at the two ladies with a large, somewhat creepy smile. "Hi. How are you ladies today? How can I help you? Are you here about the guy next door? Are you cops? You don't look like cops. I already talked to some cops." He spoke quickly without taking a breath.

"Easy there, big fella." Judy held up her hand in an attempt to interrupt the smiling man's rambling. "We are here to ask you about Ron Castle, but we are not cops."

"Oh, good. Not that I have anything against cops. I like cops, just like anyone else. All the same, I'm glad you're not cops. They have a lot of questions. Would you ladies like some tea? I have chamomile. I love chamomile. I think I have fresh lemons." His eyes were wide, and he managed to keep smiling the entire time he spoke.

As the tall smiling man drew in a breath, Lily decided to get a few words in. "My name is Lily Pine, and this is my daughter Judy. We'd like to ask you about what happened here early this morning."

"I'm Woody, Woodrow Freeman. Are you sure you aren't cops?" The man started again.

Judy held up her press badge and interjected before he could go on. "I'm with the *Seattle Times*. We just want to know if you saw or heard anything between two and five this morning."

"That's what the cops asked me," he started again. "I was awake. I don't sleep much. I like to watch old TV shows. There was a *Twilight Zone* marathon last night. They played the episodes in order. It lasted all night long. It was great. Do you know the one where the guy is the only person left on Earth, and he collects all of the books? That one is my favorite."

Lily nodded but did not interrupt Woody. She smiled at Judy and raised her eyebrows to make sure Judy didn't interrupt again.

He continued his dissertation. "The marathon started at midnight. After the first three episodes, I had to turn the TV up. Gunfire, machine guns, hand grenades, and helicopters. It was too loud."

"There was gunfire in the building?" Judy had to interrupt to ask. She shrugged at her mother, who giggled a little.

"Chase and Ron have their TV on the other side of the wall from mine. Someone was playing video games. War games. Probably Ron and his brother, Sam. They did that a lot. It was loud, so I turned up my TV.

"Episodes are thirty minutes long as I remember. That would make it around one thirty when the war games started." Lily ascertained.

"That would be about right," Woody confirmed. "Barbara Jean Trenton was the star who watched her own old movies over and over. The gunfire was blaring over her movie at the beginning of episode four. Must have been just after one thirty."

"How long did they play games?" Judy asked.

"Well, it was after Martin picked up his car near the end of episode five. Did you know that Ron Howard was in that episode? He played Martin as a little boy."

"I didn't know that. That's very interesting," Lily replied. "Did you hear anything after the gunfire stopped?"

"Chase. I heard Chase screaming. He was going off about Annie. It was right in the middle of 'The Lonely'."

"The Lonely?" Judy questioned.

"Episode seven. It's one of my favorites. Chase started yelling, and I turned up the sound again. I pulled a stool up to sit right in front of the television. I know most of the lines, but I wanted to hear them. It didn't last long."

"Episode seven didn't last long?" Judy was trying to follow Woody's train of thought, which wasn't easy. He was all over the place and still talking quickly.

"The yelling didn't last long," Woody laughed as he spoke.

"Did you hear anything else that Chase said? Anything aside from Annie's name? You said he was yelling about Annie."

"No. I don't remember anything else he said. I was trying to concentrate on the show. I'm pretty sure he said 'Annie'. I noticed that because I like Annie. She's always very nice to me. She brings me pie from the café sometimes. She's very pretty, too." Woody blushed slightly as he spoke.

"What did he say about Annie?" Lily asked.

"I don't know. I just remember him saying her name when he was yelling," Woody responded.

"Did Ron yell back at Chase? Did you hear Ron's voice at all?" Lily asked.

"No. I didn't. I only remember hearing Chase. I thought he might have been screaming at someone on the phone. It all seemed strange." Woody pulled the door to his apartment wide open. "Where are my manners? Would you ladies like to come in? I can make some tea. I have chamomile."

"No thank you," Lily responded before Judy could open her mouth. "Does Chase yell a lot? Do you hear him through the wall often?"

"Oh, no. Chase is very quiet. That's what seemed strange. I have never heard him yell. Not until last night. Well, really it was this morning. I was watching *The Twilight Zone*. Would you like some tea? I think I have fresh lemons."

"No but thank you very much for the offer. We should be going." Lily smiled at the tall friendly man.

"One more thing," Judy said. "Do you know when Elenore Petrovsky usually gets home?"

"206. Oh, she works during the day. She usually isn't home before five, even on weekends. She doesn't like it when we turn our TVs up loud. She gets mad at us. Last night I had to turn my TV up because of the noise next door." Woody started to ramble on again.

"Yes. You told us," Judy cut him off when he took a breath, again. "We should be going. Thank you for your time."

Judy and Lily both smiled cordially at Woody and turned away from him.

"It was very nice to talk to you. Please, come again, anytime," Woody said as he closed the door.

"What do you think about that?" Judy asked her mother.

"I'm not sure how reliable his account is, but if we can trust his memory based on his television schedule it seems to follow along with Chase's story. He sounded very sure that he didn't hear Ron's voice."

"He also said that Chase was yelling at Ron about Annie. Chase said it was about the mess in the apartment."

"If Woody likes Annie, maybe he just imagined Chase was talking about Annie."

"I suppose that's possible. He has a good depiction of the timeline based on his *Twilight Zone* schedule. The fact that he repeats himself may be a problem on the witness stand."

6

Lily and Judy tried the three doors across the hall from Woody, Chase, and Elenore's apartments with no luck in finding anyone at home. Judy found an address and a home number for Ron Castle's parents and little brother by searching the internet. She dialed the number. Philip Castle answered the phone and refused to speak with Judy. Determined to learn more about the activities of Ron Castle the day before he died, Judy dug up an address for Julius Barbor. This led Judy and Lily to a small, pastel-yellow house at the edge of downtown Bainbridge Island. The adorable home was trimmed in white with small shutters and a flowerbox under each window.

Judy and Lily stood on the small front porch watching the door open slowly. A slender, young man with tattoos on both arms stepped out onto the wooden structure and closed the door behind him. He had short brown hair and a friendly smile.

"Hello. Is there something I can do for you?" He said.

"We are looking for Julius Barbor," Judy stated.

"I'm Juice Barbor. How can I help you?"

"We are here on behalf of Chase Raker. Did you hear about Ron Castle?" Lily asked.

"I heard from, his brother Sam, that Ron was found dead this morning... which is crazy because we were just with him," Juice said.

"What do you mean?" Judy asked.

"Well, I was out with Sam last night. We decided to stop off at Ron's before we went home. He's always up late. We had a beer and played a video game. Nothing out of the ordinary." His smiling face turned melancholy.

"Was Ron okay when you left?" Judy asked.

"Yes. He turned off the game and started surfing channels. The guy literally stays up all night," Juice added. He let us grab some cold pizza from the box on the counter, and we left."

"Did you see Chase Raker last night?" Lily asked.

"No. That wasn't out of the ordinary either. Chase is rarely there when we drop by. Ron often commented that he only had to pay half of the rent even though he lived alone. He didn't care much that Chase wasn't around. They weren't the best of friends. Ron didn't have many friends. He was a bit abrasive." Juice squinted slightly as if he had said something harsh.

"In what way was he abrasive?" Judy wanted to understand.

"Ron was known to say inappropriate things at inappropriate times. He seemed to like to make other people uncomfortable. He was always making comments about how pretty Annie was, right in front of Chase. Chase didn't like it. He didn't bring Annie around much when he knew Ron was home. I've been friends with Sam since we were kids. I'm immune to Ron's BS." Juice smirked.

"Did anything else happen while you and Sam were at Ron's apartment? Did anyone come by? Did Ron receive any calls? Did you three fight about anything?"

"No. It was uneventful. We played *Crime Wars* for forty-five minutes or so and then Sam and I took off. Sam decided he needed to get some sleep. He was supposed to go to the beach with his girlfriend this morning. He's not at the beach of course. Since the cops called about Ron, he's been upset with himself for leaving so early last night. Well, this morning. If we had stayed longer, maybe this wouldn't have happened."

"Or, you may have all been killed," Judy replied.

"I suppose." Juice hung his head and sighed. "It's very unsettling to think about him being gone after we were at his place moments before he died. I've never known anyone who's died before. Well, not counting old people. My grandpa died when I was a kid."

"I'm sorry for your loss," Lily offered. "I'm sure this is traumatic for you since you were close to Ron."

"I'm close to Sam," Juice said as he met Lily's eyes. "I feel horrible for him. He loved his brother."

"Do you know of anyone who would want to hurt Ron?" Judy asked.

"In general, Ron wasn't well-liked," Juice stated. "That being said, I don't know of anyone who would hate him enough to kill him. I can't imagine why anyone would do such a thing."

"What did Ron spend time doing, other than working and playing video games?" Lily asked.

"Ron liked to watch horror movies and drink beer. He was into outdoor activities, but he wasn't what I would consider outdoorsy. He kayaked and did some mountain biking. Sam and I went on a couple of charter fishing trips with him out of Westport. He liked to fish for tuna. It's fun. If you haven't tried it, you should. We each hauled in our limit last time we went."

"Did Ron have a girlfriend? Any other friends he hung out with regularly?" Judy questioned.

"Ron went out on dates once in a while. Nothing that lasted. I'm not sure he had many second dates. As I said, he can be abrasive. He had quite a crush on Chase's girlfriend, Annie. She stayed clear of him."

"Do you think Chase would have tried to hurt Ron for any reason?" Lily was starting to think Juice might fuel the prosecutor's case.

"I've known Chase for a couple of years now. Sam, Ron, and I met him through the bike club at the cycling shop downtown. He's a great guy. He may be the friendliest person I've ever met. Agreeing to sign a lease with Ron was likely a mistake. I'm sure Ron wasn't easy to live with, but Chase would never hurt anyone. Chase took everything on the chin... with a smile. He always assumed positive intent and gave everyone the benefit of the doubt." Juice nodded in affirmation of his reference to Chase's character.

"Even Ron?" Judy asked.

"Yes." Juice continued to nod. "I've never heard Chase so much as raise his voice to Ron. They seemed to ignore one another for the most part."

"We appreciate you taking the time to talk with us," Lily said to the thin, young man.

"Yes. Thank you," Judy added. "Nice body art. Who does your work?"

"The Stick and Poke on Madison. Best place in town for tats," he responded, proudly holding up his arms. Sam and Ron have had work done there as well. They haven't spent as much there as I have, but we all have some unique designs from that place."

"Yes. Very nice work," Lily complimented. "We should be going. We appreciate your time."

"It was nice meeting you both. I hope everything works out okay for Chase." He smiled and opened the door slowly as the two women walked away.

7

—·—

"This is convenient," Judy said to Lily as they parked on Madison Street in Bainbridge Island's quaint downtown area. The bike shop is just a block from the tattoo parlor. Let's ask about Ron at the tattoo place first and then walk down to the bike shop. It's a small town. It's very likely someone will know who Ron is."

"Yes. Bainbridge Island is very cool. You usually come over here to catch the ferry to Seattle, don't you?"

"Yes. It's only about a thirty-minute ferry ride from here. The Bremerton ferry takes fifty minutes, and I hate driving all the way around. Riding the ferry is peaceful and scenic, so I sometimes take the longer ride from Bremerton even though the drive time only saves me ten minutes." Staring out over the water, Judy paused for a brief moment. "I love the views of the city from here. If they have a bike club here, I imagine they do road rides as well as mountain biking. I bet the bike shop organizes some rides along the coast, so the riders are able to enjoy the view. Maybe Linda and I can join the club."

"Do you think you two can keep up with club riders?" Lily asked.

"We ride at a decent speed. We like to ride along the shore in Port Orchard. It's nice and flat there. The inclines promise to be a bit more challenging here on the island. Maybe they have a beginner's ride," Lily said with a chuckle as the two ladies entered the tattoo parlor.

"Welcome, ladies," came a greeting from a smoky woman's voice.

Lily looked up to see a lady, over six feet tall, stepping through a set of beads at the entrance to the parlor's sitting room. She wore a floral print tank top and bell bottoms. She had braids in her hair and brown moccasins on her feet. Her skin was pale where it showed. Her arms and neck were covered in colorful tattoos. Most of her body art depicted jungle animals. "Hi," Lily responded.

"Hello," Judy said, also looking up at the woman who greeted them.

"We have a mother-daughter special today. Buy one get one half off," the tall lady said with a grin.

"What do you think, Mom? Should we get matching tattoos while we're here?"

"I don't think so, Judy." Lily rolled her eyes at her daughter.

"Are you sure? A pirate ship on your chest or a panther on your back?" The smiling artist grinned at Judy, thinking she was certain Lily hadn't come in for any such tattoo.

Judy laughed and said, "I'm Judy Pine. You guessed correctly. This is my mom. Her name is Lily. I'm with the *Seattle Times*. We wanted to ask you a few questions about a customer of yours, Ron Castle. Do you know him?" She spoke as if he were still alive. She wondered if the tattoo artist knew Ron was dead.

"My name is Donna. I know Ron. His little brother, Sam, has had quite a bit of work done here. Sam and his friend Juice hang out downtown all the time. They stop by to chat with us on occasion and talk to the other customers. They like to help people pick out artwork."

"What about Ron? Do you see much of him? I understand he's been in for some custom work as well." Lily was happy to move on from the topic of her being poked with a needle.

"Ron has a couple of tattoos. One on each shoulder. He doesn't have near as much of my work on him as Sam and Juice do."

"Have you or anyone else here ever had any kind of run-in with Ron Castle?" Judy asked as she admired a leopard tattoo that stretched from Donna's elbow to her neck.

"Jimmy kicked him out one time for being overly drunk," Donna responded. "It wasn't what I would call a run-in. Hey, Jimmy!" she yelled, turning her head back towards the beaded doorway.

The plastic beads clacked in a sort of rhythm as a man standing at least six inches taller than Donna ducked his way through the doorway. He had arms the size of the average man's thighs and broad muscular shoulders. He had tattoos of cartoon characters up both arms and was dressed similarly to Donna.

"What's up, babe?" he asked as he entered the room.

"These ladies are wondering about altercations involving Ron Castle," Donna responded.

"That little weasel is a pain in my neck," the large man stated. "Sam is a great guy, but Ron is an annoying drunk."

"Was," Judy stated. "I guess you haven't heard. He passed away early this morning."

"What?" Donna looked confused. "He was in his twenties. What happened to him?"

"It looks like he suffered some kind of head injury," Lily added.

"I didn't mean to speak badly of the dead. It's just that he wasn't a nice guy." Jimmy seemed embarrassed.

"Wait a minute. You aren't trying to pin something on my Jimmy, are you?" The tall, fair-skinned lady started to sound defensive.

"No. Not at all," Judy spoke up quickly. "I'm just trying to find out more about Ron. We aren't police officers. Julius Barbor told us Ron came here and to the bike store down the street with him. I'm just following up."

"I'm a lover, not a fighter," Jimmy said as he pointed to a large tattoo on his left bicep, displaying Pepé le Pew with a rose in his mouth and a heart over his head.

"I see that," Judy said with a chuckle.

"Is there anything else you can tell us about Ron, Sam, or Juice?" Lily asked as she moved towards the exit. "Do you know of anyone who might have wanted to harm him?"

"I'm sorry to hear about Ron," Donna offered. "I didn't like the guy all that much, but he didn't deserve to die so young. We didn't know him very well. I'm sorry, I don't think I can help you."

"Yeah. That sucks," Jimmy agreed with a shrug.

Judy and Lily walked out into the sunlight and ventured towards the bike shop that was an easy walk from where they had met Donna and Jimmy. A buzzer sounded as Lily and Judy entered the large shop.

"Welcome to Bainbridge Bikes. Can I help you ladies with anything in particular?" A small, thin man appearing to be close to sixty moved from behind a display counter. He wore fitted bike shorts and a bright red, riding jersey with the store name stretched across his chest.

"Yes, we were hoping to get some information about Ron Castle. We understand he has ridden with your club. Do you know him?" Judy smiled broadly at the gray-haired man.

"Yes. I know Ron. He rides with us once in a while. Did he recommend the shop? Are you two looking to do some cycling? I'm Greg Willis, the owner. I go on most of the organized rides."

"I'm Judy Pine, and this is my mom, Lily. I am interested in hearing about your organized rides. I'm a beginner, but I love to ride. I have a nice Scott bike I picked up in Ohio." Lily thought she might get more information from Greg if he viewed her as a potential customer. "It needs a once-over. I haven't ridden much since I moved here."

"We have a beginner's ride group, but Ron isn't in that one. He sets a bad example for some of our newer riders, so we try to keep him out of our novice group even though he isn't a very experienced rider." Greg raised his eyebrows and rubbed his forehead nervously.

"What makes him a bad example?" Lily asked.

"He doesn't follow our safety guidelines. Ron acts like every ride is a race. He's constantly passing riders without a word. He takes the downhills too fast and doesn't always wear a helmet. He rides off ahead of the group quite a bit. Not user-friendly for new riders, that's all. He hasn't ridden with any of our groups in months. I'm surprised he sent you here."

"I'm sorry. I wasn't clear. He didn't recommend we come here. We were hoping to learn about Ron and Chase from some of the people around town who are familiar with them. Julius Barbor suggested you might be able to help us." Judy admitted.

"So, you aren't here to get information about rides and bike setup?" The shop owner looked puzzled.

"She is interested in cycling, but that is an aside," Lily interjected. "Ron was found dead in his apartment early this morning. Chase Raker has been arrested in conjunction with the death. We are hoping to help Chase."

"Why didn't you say so in the first place?" Greg's eyes widened. "Chase is a great guy. Why has he been arrested? The cops don't think he caused Ron's death, do they?"

"They do. We are hoping to prove otherwise. Can you help us? Will you tell us what you know about the two young men?" Lily asked with soulful eyes.

"Ron's a bit standoffish. He's a loner, and most people leave him alone. Well, except for his brother, Sam. Sam is the one who brought Ron in here and got him started riding. Sam and Juice have been riding with us since they were young teens. I didn't mean to imply Ron was a bad person. He's just a bit reckless. We all had our faults when we were young. I'm sorry to hear that he didn't get a chance to grow out of his arrogance. No one should get cheated out of the years they have coming. We should all get to grow wrinkles, meet our grandchildren, and let go of our regrets." Greg shook his head sullenly.

"Grandchildren. There's an interesting topic," Lily said as she grinned at Judy.

"I guess you should have had more kids," Judy jested. "Did you ever witness Chase or anyone else being aggressive towards Ron Castle? Do you know of anyone who would want to hurt him?"

"I haven't seen Ron for several months. Chase was in here last week with his girlfriend. They tried out a few bikes. He's hoping to get her into cycling. He implied that he was going to buy her a bike." Greg looked through the two ladies as he tapped his lips with his index finger. "Annie. Yes, I think her name was Annie."

"Yes. Chase does date a girl named Annie," Lily confirmed. "I didn't know she was considering cycling."

"Sam and Juice were here last Saturday. We rode the Chilly Hilly route," Greg said.

"What's that?" Judy asked.

"Cascade Bicycle Club has an organized ride here on the island every year in February. It's a thirty-three-mile ride along the shore. It's a great ride boasting views of the Seattle skyline. We ride the route quarterly. People come from all over for the February ride." Greg oozed with enthusiasm as he described the event.

"Did Sam's brother, Ron, ride with you last Saturday?" Judy asked.

"No," Greg responded. "We had about two dozen riders, but Ron didn't come. Neither did Chase. I asked Chase about it when he came in with Annie. He said he had to work."

"That would be her fault," Judy pointed at her mother.

"You must be the nice lady who owns the restaurant on the water over in Poulsbo." Greg looked as if a light bulb had gone off in his head. "Chase speaks fondly of you."

"That is very nice to hear." Lily blushed a little.

"Anything else you can offer about Chase or Ron?" Judy asked Greg.

"Nothing I can think of. What about the bike setup? Was that all an act to get me talking?" Greg grinned at Judy.

"Not at all. I live in Silverdale. I really do have a sweet Scott bike. I'll bring it over for a tune-up. I'm not great at maintenance. I'm interested in learning more about mountain biking as well. I've never ridden off-road."

"It's great fun. It's a whole other beast. Two very different types of riding. Maybe we can get you on a loaner sometime for a first ride to see how you like it," he offered.

"That's very kind of you. I'd like that." Judy fished a card from her purse and handed it to the man. "Let me know when you have your next novice ride. My phone number and email address are on the card.

"I'll add you to our email list. Don't give me too much credit for being nice; we sell a lot of bikes this way," Greg said with a cackle.

"Thank you for your time, Mr. Willis." Lily and Judy walked towards the door.

"Any time," he said. "Please come again."

8

Lily and Judy enjoyed a late lunch at a waterfront restaurant. They had lived on this beautiful northwestern Washington peninsula for almost two years but never failed to appreciate any opportunities to enjoy views of the water and the mountains whenever possible. After eating and forcing themselves away from the exquisite view of the Puget Sound, Lily and Judy decided to make a second stop at Chase's apartment building to attempt to talk to any of the other neighbors who may be at home now. It wasn't late enough in the day to catch Elenore Petrovsky by Woody's estimation, but they hoped to talk with the neighbors on the other side of the hall.

The two ladies entered Building Two of the complex and Judy knocked sternly on the door labeled 201. As they waited for an answer to the knock, the door to apartment 205 opened and a small woman with long, gray hair stepped out into the hallway, locking the door behind her. She glanced at Lily and Judy but only for a second. She turned towards the exit and started to move away from them.

"Excuse me," Lily said, causing the gray-haired lady to turn around. "Could we talk with you for a minute?"

The door in front of Judy opened and an average-height girl looking to be in her late teens or early twenties stood before her. "Can I help you?"

"We were hoping to find out if either of you heard anything from across the hall early this morning." Judy looked back and forth from the teenager to the older lady. "I'm Judy Pine, and this is my mother, Lily."

"Mrs. Bell, do you know these women," The girl asked.

"No. I can't say I've ever seen them before. The police have already questioned all of us." The gray-haired lady hoisted her large purse to her shoulder and leaned against the wall.

"As she said, we already answered questions about Ron and Chase this morning. You two don't look like cops." The girl studied Lily and Judy's faces as if she were deciding if she should be talking with them.

"Chase Raker works for me. He's a friend of mine. He has been arrested and we are hoping to help him," Lily thought some truth would help pave the way for a better conversation.

"Chase is a very nice young man," Mrs. Bell said with a soft smile.

"You should have led with that. I'm happy to help Chase in any way I can. He and Annie are both super sweet. Why has he been arrested? They don't think he had something to do with Ron's death, do they?" The girl's expression turned concerned.

"We can't go into all of the details, but it will help Chase if you can tell us anything you know about what happened here early this morning," Lily responded.

"Between two and five," Judy added.

"The police were here early this morning when I was on my way out. I'm retired, but I like to get out early for a walk," Mrs. Bell said. "I didn't hear anything before then. I use a CPAP machine. I don't hear much once I go to bed."

"I saw Sam and Juice going into the apartment, but I'm pretty sure that was before two. I had a study session with a friend at the all-night diner down by the ferry. We finished up around one thirty. I saw Sam and Juice going into Chase and Ron's as I came down the hall when I got home. I think I was in bed by two. That's what I told the cops, too. I'm sorry, but I don't think I'm much help either. The cops asked if I heard any yelling or anything that sounded like a struggle, but I didn't hear anything. I went to bed and didn't wake up until an officer knocked on my door this morning. I had a group project to work on after that, so I was over in Seattle. I just got home about an hour ago. There was crime tape on the door, and the police had all cleared out. By the way, my name is Valarie. Valarie Marshal."

"It sounds like you like Chase and Annie," Lily spoke to Valarie. "Since you know Sam and Juice by name, I assume you also knew Ron."

"Not a fan," Valarie replied.

"What do you mean by that?" Judy asked.

"Ron Castle was a dick. He's was not a nice guy. He's was rude and condescending. I didn't like him." Valarie spoke in a manner of fact tone.

"Don't mince any words, Valarie," the older lady chuckled.

"Did you know Ron Castle?" Lily shifted her attention to Mrs. Bell.

"Not well, but I wasn't a fan either," she gave Lily a sheepish grin.

"Sam is a sweetheart... and cute," Valarie added.

"Did you talk to Sam or Juice when you saw them early this morning?" Judy asked.

"No. I caught a glimpse of them going in the door, but they didn't see me. I didn't say anything. I was on a mission to get some sleep," she responded.

"Your neighbor in 202 said they played video games until after two and then left," Judy commented.

"Woody? He's a riot. He may not be the most reliable of witnesses. He forgets things. He repeats himself a lot. Very nice man, just a bit unstable." Valarie looked to Mrs. Bell for confirmation.

"Woody has lived there for years," Mrs. Bell added. "He slips a little more every year. When he tells you something, it's usually spot-on. He may not remember telling you, and he might tell you again... and again, but his stories are usually factual."

"It seems that Elenore Petrovsky called the police complaining about noise coming from across the hall after three o'clock. Neither of you heard anything?"

The older woman shook her head, and Valarie's expression became one of irritation as she started to talk with her hands, "Miss Petrovsky is constantly complaining. She has called the cops on Ron and Sam a couple of times before. She complains about everyone but usually not to their faces. She's a grumpy, old lady."

"Hey," Mrs. Bell interjected. "She's a good bit younger than I am."

"A good bit crabbier too." Valarie smiled at Mrs. Bell.

"She is an ill-tempered type. One of those people you shouldn't ask how they are doing. It's all bad all of the time. She complains about everything," Mrs. Bell admitted.

"Is there anything else you two can tell us about the men in 204 or who may have wanted to harm Ron Castle?" Judy asked.

"Any number of people may have wanted to do harm to Ron, but I doubt anyone would go to the trouble of killing him. He's not worth the aggravation," the college girl said.

"I don't know any of them well. I said hello to them when I saw them. Chase is kind and sometimes helps me carry things to my door. I can't say Ron was as helpful, but I had no reason to dislike him. I don't know the other boys. I have seen them come and go, but I've never interacted with them," Mrs. Bell stated.

"Thank you both for your time," Lily offered. "Do you happen to know if anyone is home at the apartment between yours?"

"Dylan Hart lives there. He isn't here much. I haven't seen him at all today," Valarie said.

"The police asked about him when they questioned me," Mrs. Bell added. I don't think they got a chance to speak with him.

Judy knocked on the door in the middle of the hall hoping Mr. Hart might be in there. The four women remained silent for over a minute. Judy shrugged her shoulders and Valarie smiled and offered a goodbye. Lily and Judy offered their thanks again and left the building behind Mrs. Bell.

9

— · —

"Hey Judy," Piper Baxter greeted Judy over her cell phone. "Did you get any useful information? I'm afraid Chase is going to be sent to Port Orchard Corrections this afternoon. He seems like a nice guy. I'm afraid he will have trouble coping with that place. It's very different from Bainbridge Island holding."

"I have you on speakerphone. My mom is here with me," Judy informed Piper. "We have a pretty firm timeline on people coming and going the morning of the murder based on a statement from one of the neighbors. We didn't get to talk to the lady who placed the complaint call, but we did talk to several of Chase's neighbors and Ron's brother's best friend."

"I understand the brother and his friend were in the apartment this morning. Is that the friend you spoke with?" Piper asked.

"Yes, Juice, the friend, said they were with Ron from before two until around two thirty. Ron was fine when they left, according to him," Judy replied.

"That narrows the timeline a little. Unless he's lying. It's possible that Juice and Sam killed Ron and left him dead on the couch where Chase saw him." Piper was structuring a way to show that someone besides Chase had the opportunity to kill Ron.

"I guess that's a possibility," Judy admitted.

"If this goes to court, we just need to raise reasonable doubt. I'm looking at anything we can use to poke holes in the prosecutor's case naming Chase as the only possible killer," Piper said.

"It might not be too hard. No one we talked to seemed to have fond feelings for Ron. He wasn't well-liked. The guy at the tattoo parlor once threw him out for being drunk and obnoxious. The bike shop owner said he tried to keep Ron away from new riders because he was a bad influence. His neighbor across the hall said he was a dick," Judy stated abruptly.

"Judy!" Lily exclaimed.

"Well, isn't that what she said?" Judy reacted.

"Yes, but you shouldn't say it." Lily blushed slightly.

"No matter how you say it, he wasn't considered to be much of a sweetheart, I guess," Piper interjected. "That's good. If we can show that most people who knew Ron Castle didn't like him, it will be easier to build a case for someone other than Chase killing him. Nice work, ladies. I appreciate your help."

"We are just getting started," Judy said. "We haven't talked to Elenore Petrovsky or Dylan Hart yet. We need to keep asking questions. I'm sure there is more to learn about this morning than we know at this point. A young man is dead, and we don't know why. We will keep asking questions until we reveal the truth. Even if Ron was a *dictator* without the *tator*," she paused to grin at her mom. Lily shook her head in disapproval. "He didn't deserve to die for it."

"Who is Dylan Hart?" Piper asked.

"He's another one of the neighbors in Building Two of the complex. He's the only one in the building we haven't talked to except for Elenore Petrovsky. It seems Ron and Chase were the only tenants to have two occupants in their apartment." Judy responded.

"Not surprising," Piper responded. "According to the floor plan only the middle apartments have two bedrooms. The apartments on either end only have one bedroom."

"Did you hear from Annie Beazley?

"Who is Annie Beazley?" Piper seemed confused.

"Chase's girlfriend," Judy responded.

"No. Chase hasn't said anything about a girlfriend. Maybe he doesn't want to involve her or maybe he doesn't want her to know he's in jail," Piper speculated.

"I expected her to show up at the police station to try to see him. I wonder where she ran off to if it wasn't to see Chase?" Lily pondered out loud.

"No one at the station said anything about a girl showing up on his behalf. I'll ask around to be sure," Piper offered.

"Cute little thing, dark hair, small build. She's kind of quiet." Judy described her.

"Okay. Oh, I almost forgot to tell you. The coroner said there were some red fibers in the wound on Chase's head. It could point us to a weapon. Large, blunt, and red. Nothing like that was found at the scene."

"Another piece of the puzzle. I need to get back to work, so we are on our way back to Poulsbo. Judy has work to do as well." Lily smiled as she spoke.

"Yes, Mother. We both have work to do," Judy said in a mocking tone.

"I appreciate the follow-up. Can we get together when you aren't driving so that I can get the details from your conversations with Julius and the neighbors? I want to make sure I have the timeline accurately drawn up."

"I'll try to get back to the apartment complex tonight," Judy said. "I hope to catch Elenore and Dylan at home later. I'd also like to get a chance to talk with Sam Castle. His dad turned us away when we called the house, but I'm sure I can find a cell number for Sam if I dig a little more."

"Let me know when you come back to the island. If I have time, I'll tag along. I wouldn't mind talking to Sam Castle and his family myself," Piper stated.

"I'll call you," Judy responded.

"Thanks," Piper said as she ended the call.

10

Judy dropped her mother off at Marty's on the Bay, and Lily hurried inside to check on the dinner shift preparations. Lily asked David to join her in the office after she greeted all of the evening staff.

"What's going on Lily? How is Chase? Did he get out?" David questioned her.

"We weren't able to get him out of jail, yet. He's being transferred to Port Orchard. We won't be expecting him in for work for the next few days. Please try to staff the kitchen accordingly."

"No problem. I was supposed to be off for the next two days. I'll cover Chase's shifts. Is there anything I can do to help Chase?"

"Is there anything else you can tell me about last night... this morning? Did Chase say anything about Ron or talk to him on the phone while you were with him? Did anything out of the ordinary happen while you were out with Chase?"

"Nothing out of the ordinary at all. We had quite a few beers and some tequila shots. We had to run to catch the last ferry to the Island. If we had missed it, Annie would have killed us. Sorry, poor choice of words. Annie dropped us at the Bremerton ferry after work. We took the ferry to Seattle and started drinking after we had pizza at Pike's Market. Next thing you know, it was time to catch the Bainbridge Island ferry, and we were a half mile away. We ran to the pier. Made it just in time. The ride was quiet. Not many people, thankfully. We were able to stretch out on some benches for the ride. We talked about getting a beer on the boat, but we were so winded after the run, we weren't up for it."

"So, you reclined on some benches and rode to Bainbridge, and then, you parted ways to go to your respective homes?"

"Yes. That pretty much sums it up. From work to the Bremerton ferry to Seattle to the Bainbridge ferry and home. Pizza and a lot of adult beverages in the middle."

"Did you two talk with other people at the bars or on the ferry?"

"Sure, we did. We talked to the pizza guy and a couple who sat next to us at the market. We talked to some guys at one of the bars. One of them made a comment about the Thrashers jersey I had on, and we got to talking about Atlanta. Other than that, we talked to each other, I guess.

It gets a little fuzzy towards the end of the night." He smiled broadly.

"Did he talk on the phone at all? Did you leave him alone at any point during the evening?"

"We were within feet of each other all night aside from restroom breaks. The more you drink the more you have to go to the men's room, you know. He was on the phone on the way back on the ferry. I'm pretty sure he was talking to Annie. It was just before we docked, so we didn't talk much after. I don't know for sure that it was her. I may have assumed that no one else would talk to him at that hour." David laughed.

Lily smiled. "You are probably right. I'll ask Annie once I catch up to her. I've tried calling her a few times today. She doesn't answer. She hasn't been to the police station. Have you spoken to her?"

"No. I've been pretty busy here, but I haven't had any missed calls today. She knows Chase was arrested, right?"

"Yes. I told her right after Chase called me. I haven't talked to her since. She got Tonia to come in to take over her shift at Virgil's, and she left. I thought we'd see her at the station, but no one has seen her there. I'll check with Virgil. If you hear from her, will you ask her to call me? I'm worried about her."

"Will do. I'm sorry I wasn't more help."

"Thanks for talking through it with me."

11

J udy went back to Lily's house to feed and walk the dogs. They had called Wendy, Lily's dog walker, earlier to ask that she spend some time with the dogs around lunchtime. She had walked them all and commented on how adorable Jack was. Jed knocked on the door shortly after Judy arrived.

"Hey Judy, where's Lily?" Jed asked.

"She had to stop by the restaurant. I don't think she expected you to be back this soon. I guess you missed Brick so much you had to leave the food show early." She giggled.

"Yes, that's it," he said with a smile. "I do miss the big guy." Brick jumped almost straight up in the air with excitement when he saw Jed entering the condo.

"I guess he missed you, too. I don't understand how he jumps like that. It seems to defy all laws of physics."

"He's a special dog." Jed got down on one knee and scratched the large dog's neck as Brick rubbed his large head against Jed's face. Jack ran around the two barking at a high pitch. "Who's this little man?"

"That is Jack. He's my special guy."

"It's nice to finally meet you, Jack. I've heard good things." Jed picked the small dog up and cradled him in one arm while he scratched Jack behind his ear with one finger. "Where's your BMW?"

"I traded it in for a Jeep Wrangler. The way everyone obeys the speed limits around here, having a sportscar seemed pointless. I'm trying to fit in." She snickered. "You have some clients on Bainbridge Island, right?"

"Sure. I have a truck over there every day. We do a substantial amount of business on the island. Why?"

"Did Mom tell you about Chase being arrested?"

"No. What's that about?"

"His roommate, Ron Castle, is dead. They have arrested Chase on suspicion of murder."

"Do the police have witnesses, a motive, or a weapon? Why do they think Chase did it?"

"A neighbor heard Chase screaming at Ron and called the police. When the officers arrived, they found Ron dead on the couch."

"I can't believe Chase would do such a thing." Jed put Jack on the sofa and sat down on the floor next to Nellie to rub her belly.

"No one can. Well, no one except for the police. I should have said, 'No one who knows Chase.'"

"Can you ask around to see if any of your customers know the two guys and can supply any information about their relationship? It would also be helpful if anyone could tell us why someone might want to murder Ron Castle."

"I can ask around. Is this information out to the public?"

"It seems to be no secret that Ron is dead, and that Chase has been arrested."

"So, no scoop on your part?"

"I'm hoping to get the story about how the police arrested the wrong man without doing a proper investigation."

"Always making friends with law enforcement," he spoke with a sarcastic tone.

"I'm friendly with the smart cops," she cackled. "I need to do some work, but you are welcome to stay a while and wait for Mom to get home. She was just checking on the schedules and picking up her SUV. She should be along soon."

"Thanks, but I should get on home and get settled for the night. "He stood and clicked a leash on Brick's collar. "I have a long day of catch-up tomorrow. Thank your mom for watching Brick for me and tell her to call when she gets time. I'll give you a ring if I learn anything from my Bainbridge Island clients. Nice to meet you, Jack." He smiled at the small dog and opened the door, being careful not to let the little guy out.

"Okay, thanks," Judy offered as she picked Jack up and closed the door gently behind Jed.

12

J udy stared at the black 206 in the middle of the door, finding it interesting that there were no peepholes in the doors in the complex. A nuance she hadn't noticed earlier. She knocked a second time.

"Who is it?" came loudly from the other side of the door.

"Judy Pine. I'm with the *Seattle Times*. I'd like to ask you a few questions."

The door opened swiftly. "It's been quite a bit quieter without those boys next door." Mrs. Petrovsky spoke in a loud voice.

"Are you talking about Chase Raker and Ron Castle?"

"Yes. Noise. Noise. Noise. Always noise coming from over there. They disturb my sleep. I couldn't listen to any more of it last night. First the banging and shooting. The TV was blaring and then Chase started yelling. I should have called the police sooner. That boy might still be alive if I would have complained sooner." She stopped talking long enough to take a few breaths.

"Could you tell that Chase was yelling at *Ron*?" Judy wanted to keep the lively lady talking.

"Who else would he be yelling at?"

"Do you know for sure that it was Chase doing the shouting?"

"It was Chase. I'm sure of that."

"Did Ron scream back at him? Did they exchange words?"

"I could only hear Chase, but I assumed he was likely just closer to the door. With the TV turned up so loud, I may not have been able to hear Ron from the other side of the room."

"Was it Ron and Chase's television that was loud or was it Woody's?"

"They both play their TVs so loud. It's hard to say for sure. All I know is that Chase was yelling. By the time I got off the phone with the cops, he had stopped. I could still hear the TV. The police didn't show up for hours."

"Did you hear Chase leave? Did the door slam? Did you hear footsteps? Anything?"

"No. I had no idea he had left. I stayed in my apartment until the police officer knocked on my door. I watched them pull the gurney out with the sheet over the boy. The police told me it was Ron."

"Did you talk to any of the neighbors at the time of the incident or while the police were here?"

"No. I heard the police knocking on doors and talking with people. I went to bed. I didn't talk to anyone other than the nice officer who came to my door."

"Could you make out what Chase said? Do you know what he was shouting about?"

"Nothing that made any sense."

"What did you hear? Tell me. Even if it doesn't make sense, it might be helpful."

"Helpful to your story? Will you print what I say? Even if it doesn't make sense? It'll make me sound like a crazy person."

"I won't print anything you don't agree to."

"No. I don't trust you. Reporters print what they want. They misquote people all the time."

"I won't. I promise. Besides, I'm more concerned about proving Chase didn't kill Ron. That's more important than a newspaper story. Anything you know might help me get to the truth of what happened."

"He sounded extremely mad. He was yelling like a crazy person."

"What did he say, Mrs. Petrovsky? Please. Tell me what you heard."

"Torch my grandma. I'll kill you."

"'I'll kill you.' Are you sure that's what he said?"

"That's what I heard. I know. It doesn't make any sense. Why would he tell Ron to torch his grandma?"

"Did you tell this to the police?"

"I told the police officer that he said, 'I'll kill you,' but not the other part."

"Did you hear him say anything else?"

"No. That's when I had enough. I went to get my phone to call the police. It was in the bedroom. I called from my bedroom so that I could hear the person on the phone better."

"Did you hear or see anyone other than Chase? Was there anyone in the hall? Did you notice anyone else enter or leave the building late last night?"

"No. I didn't leave my apartment. I didn't see anyone. I didn't open my door. I heard it all through the walls. The walls are very thin here. Those boys are always loud. I hear them through the wall."

"Thank you, Mrs. Petrovsky. Thank you very much. You have been especially helpful. Chase's lawyer, Piper Baxter, may want to speak with you. Would that be all right with you?"

"I guess it would. Are you going to tell her what I told you?"

"Yes. Don't worry. I don't think you are crazy, and neither will she. It will be okay. I'll be in touch."

"Okay. Goodnight."

Elenore Petrovsky stepped inside her apartment and closed the door. Judy heard the deadbolt turn in the door frame. As she started to jot some notes in her pad, the door across the hall opened slowly. Mrs. Bell peered through the gap in the door with a smirk on her wrinkled face.

"Hi, Mrs. Bell," Judy said softly.

"She is a little crazy," Mrs. Bell whispered and then closed the door as carefully as she had opened it.

"Wait. Mrs. Bell," Judy called after the old woman as she wrapped her knuckles on Mrs. Bell's door.

Mrs. Bell did not respond. She didn't come back to the door at Judy's request, so Judy moved on to apartment 203, Dylan Hart's apartment. She knocked boldly on the door. No one came. She knocked louder, but still, no one answered from inside door 203. Judy heard another door open behind her. She turned to find Woody standing in the hall. His door was wide open, and Judy could hear Ron Howard and Henry Winkler in the background.

"Woody, are you watching *Happy Days*?" Judy asked with a bit of a giggle.

"I am. Would you like to come in and watch it with me? I'll make some tea."

Judy approached Woody as he backed into the small apartment. She wanted to see the television and how it was positioned on the wall. She thought it best to stay in the hall. She stopped in the doorway. She smiled at seeing the characters from the old comedy show. The television rested in the middle of the wall Woody shared with apartment 202. She pictured Ron and Chase's living room in her mind as looking similar to Woody's with their TV on the other side of the wall she was looking at. That meant it was not on the wall nearest Elenore Petrovsky's apartment. Judy surmised that Chase and Ron were likely close to the wall they shared with Elenore when she heard Chase last night.

"It's late. I should get back to Silverdale. I was wondering if you remembered anything more about what we talked about earlier today."

"I remember you. I don't know what we talked about, but I remember you. You're pretty. There was another lady here with you. She's pretty, too."

"I'm Judy. I was here with Lily. You told us about the *Twilight Zone* marathon and about how you had to turn up your television because of the loud game playing next door." Judy pointed at the wall Woody shared with Chase. You told us you heard Chase yelling. Did you hear him threaten Ron?"

"I remember. I offered you some tea. You didn't come in for tea."

"Woody. Listen to me. I need to know if you heard Chase threaten Ron. I need to know if you heard Ron at all. Can you remember? Can you remember what happened during the seventh episode?" Judy flipped through her notebook quickly. "'The Lonely.' Episode seven. 'The Lonely.' Do you remember what you heard?"

"Yes. Jean Marsh was a robot. She was left on the other planet with the man who was convicted of murder."

"Not the *Twilight Zone* show, Woody. Not the show. Real life. Next door. What did you hear from Chase and Ron's apartment next door?"

"There was yelling." Woody stopped talking. A puzzled look covered his large, pale face.

"What was the yelling about? Do you remember what they said?"

"No. I'm sorry. I don't remember anything they said. I don't think I was listening. The man was on another planet, and they brought the robot woman to keep him company. Would you like some tea? I have fresh lemons."

"No thank you. It was nice to see you again. I should get going. You have a nice evening."

"You too, Judy."

Judy smiled at his remembering her name. It seems it was the only thing he remembered. That and *The Twilight Zone*.

13

"Dylan Hart?" Judy asked as she was greeted by a male voice on the other end of the phone.

"This is Dylan. Who are you?"

"My name is Judy Pine. I was hoping to ask you a few questions about Ron Castle and Chase Raker."

"Does this have to do with the crime tape across the hall and the messages I received from Detective Harris?"

"Yes. I believe it does. Are you aware of what happened across the hall from your apartment early yesterday morning?"

"I saw the crime tape. That is the beginning and end of my knowledge of anything happening in the building related to a crime. I went home to shower and get some clean clothes this morning. Other than that, I haven't been in my apartment building since two o'clock yesterday morning. My mom is in the hospital. I've been staying with her. I run home in the middle of the night to shower and get clean clothes. I'm with her now. Are you with the police department?"

"No. I'm a friend of Chase Raker's. He's been arrested for Ron Castle's murder. I'm hoping to prove he didn't kill Ron."

"Wow. I had no idea Ron was dead. Chase wouldn't have done that. Chase is a nice guy. He's a bit of a partier but a nice guy. How can I help?"

"I just need to know if you heard or saw anything yesterday when you were in the building. Didn't you say you were there around two?"

"Yes. I left the Silverdale Hospital a little before two in the morning yesterday. I drove straight home and showered. I sifted through my mail and had a quick bite to eat. Then, I drove back to Silverdale."

"Did you see or hear any of your neighbors while you were there yesterday?"

"I could hear noise coming from across the hall when I walked in."

"What kind of noise? Did it sound like people talking or yelling?"

"No. I'm pretty sure it was coming from a television. It may have been more than one television. Those guys across the hall are always up all hours of the night."

"Did you hear or see anyone?"

"I didn't hear any voices I recognized, but I saw Annie on my way out."

"You saw Annie? Annie Beazley?"

"I don't know her last name. She dates Chase. I saw her leaving the building."

"Did you talk to her?"

"No. I saw her from a distance. I walked out of the building, and she was already in the parking lot. She hurried through the parking lot and got in her car. I don't know her all that well. I don't see her at the apartment complex very often. I assumed she had been there with Chase and was going home. I didn't think much of it, to be honest."

"What time would that have been?"

"Not much before three, I wouldn't think. I wasn't in my apartment for long. A quick shower and a sandwich. I'm sure I was back on the road before three."

"Did you see or hear anyone or anything else?"

"I heard what sounded like TVs and saw Annie. Nothing else that I can remember. As I said, I wasn't there for long."

"Thank you, Dylan. This is very helpful."

"Do I need to call that detective back and tell him the same story?"

"You should, but it might help Annie and Chase if you wait a little while to do that. I don't suppose you've seen Annie since then?"

"No."

"Okay, thank you, Dylan. I appreciate you taking the time to talk with me. I hope your mother has a speedy recovery."

"Thank you."

14

Lily walked into the visiting area of the Kitsap County Jail in Port Orchard. It was a large room scattered with steel tables connected to stools that were bright orange. Most of the tables were taken by at least one visitor talking with an inmate. Lily could identify the inmates by their drab grey clothing. She spotted Chase sitting in the back of the room. Lily walked briskly towards him, trying to ignore the many conversations going on around her. She sat across from Chase and looked into his weary face.

"Lily, you shouldn't have come here. This is no place for a nice lady like you."

"*You* shouldn't be here. Are you okay? Will you be okay here for a few days if you have to remain here? I don't know when we'll be able to get you out. Miss Baxter is trying to get your bail hearing set."

"I'd be better if she can get me out of here." Chase looked past Lily, noticing Judy crossing the room.

Judy sat down next to her mother and leaned towards Chase, speaking in a whisper, "Dylan Hart saw Annie at your apartment yesterday morning. She was there before you got home. Woody heard you yelling something about Annie moments after you arrived at the apartment. Elenore Petrovsky called the police because you were yelling so loud. She said she heard you say you'd kill him. She'll likely testify to that in court. You're not telling us the whole story here. You have to come clean with us. We can't help you if we can't believe what you say."

"You should leave me here. Forget about the bail hearing. Tell Piper I want to talk to her. I want to change my plea. I did it. I'm guilty. I belong in jail. Leave me in here," he begged as he started to cry.

"Don't be silly," Lily said in a loud tone.

"Dylan barely knows Annie," Chase began to talk in the same quiet manner Judy spoke to him in. "Woody has no idea what he's talking about. He never does. Elenore is right. I said it, and I did it."

"What did you hit him with?" Judy whispered a little louder.

"What does it matter? I told you I did it. I'll sign a full confession. Get Piper in here." Chase was no longer whispering.

"If you hit Ron with something and killed him, you must know what you hit him with. Why not tell us, if you are planning to sign a confession and go to prison for it?"

"A minute ago, you wanted to get out of here. Chase, why are you doing this?" Lily asked as her eyes filled with tears and fear.

Chase stood and turned towards one of the guards. "We are done here. Please take me back to my cell."

The guard obliged, and Judy and Lily watched as Chase was led out of the room. They left the visiting area and walked out under the dark, cloud-covered sky. They didn't say a word to one another until they reached Lily's SUV.

"He's lying," Judy said with conviction.

"Why? Why would he do that?"

"I have a feeling Annie can answer that question for us. We have to find her. We've talked to all of the neighbors and Juice. We still need to talk to Sam Castle, and most of all, we need to talk to Annie Beazley. She's the key to this whole thing. She was there moments before Chase made it home Friday night. She was with Ron. I'm convinced she knows something."

"I have asked everyone I can think of about her. I don't know where else to turn."

"We need to find a way to let her know Chase is about to take the fall for something he didn't do. If she cares for him at all, that will bring her out of hiding. Let's get home. I'll work from there. I need to relieve Wendy. Jack is going to think he's Wendy's dog with all the time she's been spending with him."

"I should get back to the restaurant. Should we call Piper Baxter? Chase asked us to get her to see him."

"I think it will be for the best if we can delay that as long as possible. We need to find a way to change his mind before he signs that confession. I don't want to expedite that process by sending Piper to see him."

15

David and Linda entered the office at Marty's on the Bay. Lily was finishing up the nightly bookwork. "Thank you both for picking up the slack the last couple of days. I know it's been tough not having Chase here," Lily said.

"We appreciate you coming in to work with us again this evening," Linda offered.

"Nice of you to finish up the cash work. We'll be out of here early tonight," David added.

"Do you think Chase will be back to work soon?" Linda asked as she took a seat across the office desk from Lily.

"I don't know how long all of this is going to take. We don't have enough answers. I don't suppose either of you has any idea where we might be able to find Annie. She doesn't answer her phone, and we haven't been able to catch her at her apartment. We have reason to believe she can help us understand what happened to Ron Castle." Lily looked up at David.

"I haven't seen Annie since she dropped us at the ferry after work on Friday," David said.

"Have you checked with Virgil? She never misses work. She's very dependable. I assume you've checked the café. If she hasn't been there the past couple of days, I'd be surprised if Virgil didn't know why." Linda looked confused.

"I checked with Virgil. She left the café right after I told her about Chase being arrested. She called Virgil later that day and told him she'd need a couple of days off. He hasn't heard from her since," Lily said.

"Did you ask Tonia? Maybe Annie told her where she'd be," Linda said.

"Chase. Did you ask Chase? Annie loves Chase. She would surely be in contact with him. Is he allowed visitors? Can he make phone calls? Surely, she has spoken to him." David seemed confident.

"There has been no evidence that she has been in contact with him at all," Lily responded. "I expected her to be at the Bainbridge Island Police Station when we got there the day he was arrested. She didn't show up. We thought for sure she would be at Kitsap County Corrections once he was moved there. He *is* allowed visitors. Judy and I went to see him. He's not doing very well, I'm afraid."

"It all seems very strange that Annie hasn't visited him. Do you think something might have happened to her? Do you think whoever killed Ron Castle might have done something to Annie as well?" Linda's eyes lit up with terror.

"I don't think there's any reason to think something bad has happened to her," Lily said in a calming tone.

"I'm sure Annie is okay. Why would anyone want to hurt Annie?" David added.

"Will you both try to reach her? She might be more likely to respond to one of you," Lily requested.

"I'll try right now," Linda said as she pulled her phone from her apron pocket.

"I left my phone in my locker, but I'll give it a try too," David said.

"Annie, it's Linda Holt from Marty's. Give me a call when you get this message. Thank you." Linda hung up her phone and shook her head. "Voicemail."

"Please let me know if either of you is able to reach her. Please ask her to call me. Let's call it a night. I'll see you in the morning." Lily rose from her chair and the three restaurant workers left the office.

16

Judy awoke to pounding at her front door. Jack began to yip and growl. He seemed sure he could protect Judy from whatever was causing alarm in the middle of the night. Judy looked at the clock on her nightstand. It was almost midnight. The pounding continued as she walked through the dark house towards the front door of her Silverdale home. Judy turned on the front porch light without adding any light to the inside of the house. She wanted to have the advantage over whoever was aggressively beating on her door at this late hour. Jack continued to growl as Judy clutched him in her left arm.

Holding her phone in her right hand ready to hit send on a 911 call, Judy peered out the sidelight at her front entrance. A young man stood a few steps from the door looking up at the light that had just come on. Judy recognized the man from photos she had seen on the internet recently. It was Sam Castle.

"Judy Pine! I need to talk to you!" Sam screamed as he reached out to knock on the door again.

"Sam. What are you doing here?" she yelled through the door. Judy wanted to talk to Sam about the morning of the murder, but she wasn't sure that this was the time or the place. The tone of his voice seemed threatening to her.

"I hear you were trying to help Chase Raker. I want to talk to you."

"I don't think this is the best time for us to be doing this," Judy lowered her voice a little.

"I just found out you were involved. Juice told me. Reporters started calling right away, so we haven't been taking any calls. Juice said my dad told you you weren't welcome at our house. Juice thinks you're sincerely trying to help. Are you?"

"I want to find out what happened to your brother. I don't believe Chase killed him. I hope to prove that."

"Judy, will you open the door? I'm not here to hurt you. I want to help you. I think Chase is innocent, too. I don't know who killed my brother, but I'm sure it wasn't Chase. He doesn't have a violent bone in his body. He may be the kindest person I know."

"What about your parents? What do they think?" Judy asked as she opened the door slowly. Her little dog growled softly. "It's okay Jack," she assured him.

"I don't know why you'd be afraid to open your door to strangers in the middle of the night when you have that ferocious guard dog to protect you." Sam tried grinning, but Judy didn't look like she was in a jovial mood.

"He's watching you," she gave him a sarcastic warning. Judy turned on the inside lights and opened the door completely. "I prefer we stay right here to talk if you don't mind."

"I understand. I'm sorry if I scared you. Two-story house. I assumed I had to be loud to wake you. My dad is perfectly fine putting the blame on Chase if that's where the cops say to put it. Dad and Ron didn't get along when my brother was alive. Now, he acts like it's important to him to see Chase brought to justice. My mom just stays in bed crying. She's overcome by grief. I have no idea what she thinks. She doesn't talk to us. She just weeps constantly."

"What can you tell me about the morning your brother died?"

"I have no idea what happened after Juice and I left the apartment Friday night... well, Saturday morning. We stopped by to play video games. Ron was quiet. He didn't seem himself. I thought he was probably getting sick. He had ordered a pizza but hadn't eaten any of it. We weren't there very long. I doubt we were in his apartment for an hour. I had an early morning planned. Juice and I decided we should go home to get some sleep... I decided really. Juice doesn't require much sleep. I think he only sleeps a few hours a night. He's always happy to stay up all night. He and Ron both."

"Do you remember what time you were there?"

"Juice and I got there around one and left before two. Other than acting like he might be getting sick, Ron seemed fine when we left. He was watching TV when we got there, and he went back to it when we were leaving. He told us he had been watching TV since we dropped him off after the bike ride. That's usually what Ron did at night."

"Did you and Juice leave together?"

"Yes," Sam answered.

"Are you sure Juice didn't go back to Ron's after the two of you left?"

"I dropped him off at his house. If he had gone back to Ron's for some reason, I'm sure he would have told me. Besides, he doesn't have a car."

"He could have walked. He has a bike, right?"

"I guess it's possible, but I don't know why he would have gone back there that night. Did he tell you he went back to see Ron after we left?"

"No. I just want to cover all the bases. Juice said Ron liked to do some outdoor activities. Biking, hiking, kayaking."

"Yes, he was full-on during the day. As a matter of fact, we went mountain biking the day before he died. At night, he was a couch potato. He wasn't one for going out for any type of nightlife. He didn't even like to go out for dinner."

"Did he date much?"

"Once in a while. Not often."

"What about Annie Beazley?"

"What about Annie? What do you mean? Annie is Chase's girl."

"Did Ron have feelings for Annie? Was he ever inappropriate with her?"

"Annie is cute. Maybe too cute for Chase. We talked about how lucky Chase was and that he was dating out of his league. Harmless joking. We even told Chase that. We didn't mean anything by it. Chase didn't seem to care. He agreed with us. He seems to think he's pretty lucky to have her."

"Did your brother say anything to you and Juice about Annie or Chase on the morning in question?"

"Not that I remember. We didn't talk much. We were playing a game. We had the sound up loud. We were focused on the game. We didn't chat while we played."

"Did you see anyone else in the apartment complex while you were there? Anyone at all?"

"No. I mean, it was one in the morning. We rarely ran into any of Ron's neighbors when we stopped by late at night. I don't remember seeing anyone while we were there that morning. I didn't see anyone other than Ron and Juice. Do you think you can help Chase?"

"I'm going to do everything I can. I'm piecing things together. I was hoping you'd give me something new to go on."

"I'm sorry I wasn't much help. I feel better knowing you're working on the case. Aren't you the one who caught that guy who poisoned his uncle in Port Townsend?"

"I helped a little. You found out where I live, so I assume you know how to get in touch with me."

"Internet. You know."

"Call me if you think of anything that you haven't already told me. It might be helpful if you could get your parents to talk with me."

"I doubt there's any chance of that happening, but if you do speak with my dad, don't tell him I was here. He will view it as some type of disloyalty. He wouldn't want me to talk to anyone helping the man who killed his son. That's how he would see it."

"What about your mom? If she snaps out of her constant crying, will you ask her to call me?"

"I will, but I don't see how it will help."

"You never know."

"Okay. Thanks for talking to me, Judy."

"It's been my pleasure. Thanks for coming by. Maybe next time you could call first."

"I'll try to catch you before you go to bed too." This time, he managed to grin at her, and she returned a smile.

17

"Chase has asked me to change his plea to guilty," Piper stated with wide eyes. "What did you two say to him?" She looked across her small desk covered in file folders, hoping to get an answer from Lily or Judy.

"It has something to do with Annie," Judy stated softly as she nodded. "After I told him Dylan had seen Annie near the murder scene that night, he started talking about confessing."

"Do you think someone is threatening Annie? Maybe the killer is holding her somewhere. If that were true, Chase would do anything to save her," Lily stated.

"Even if it meant going to prison for the rest of his life?" Piper asked.

"Yes. I believe he would do anything to protect Annie," Lily responded.

"How would the killer have let Chase know he had Annie? I don't see how that's possible. Would he take the fall for her? What if Annie killed Ron? Chase could be covering for her." Judy's eyes lit up. "Doesn't it seem odd to you that she hasn't been to see him, and neither David nor Linda can get her on the phone?"

Lily looked out the window as people shuffled by on the sidewalk. She wasn't people-watching. Rather, she was running her conversation with Linda and David over in her mind. "David said he hadn't *seen* Annie since the night Ron died. He didn't call her in front of me as Linda did. His phone was in his locker. He said he would try later. He said he would try to reach her but never verbally agreed to let me know if he talked to her."

"Do you think he was lying to you?" Piper asked.

"No. I think he was trying very hard not to. It didn't register at the time, but now I'm starting to wonder if David doesn't know more than he's telling us."

"Do you think he may have been in Ron and Chase's apartment the night of the murder?" Judy asked.

"I don't know. I do think he may be able to help us find Annie," Lily said.

"If Dylan Hart is right and Annie was there, we need to talk to her. We need to find her before Chase signs a full confession," Piper said.

"Is David at work now?" Judy asked her mother.

"He is, but he's leaving soon. He has worked quite a few hours this week. Linda is letting him off early," Lily replied.

"Let's get to Poulsbo and follow him when he leaves work. Maybe we'll get lucky, and he'll lead us to Annie," Judy suggested.

"I have to go see Chase in Port Orchard. My client is asking to confess to murder. I can't put off meeting with him much longer." Piper stood and extended her hands as if she were giving up.

"I'll go with you. Maybe I can talk some sense into him," Lily said.

"Tell him about all the people we have interviewed. Tell him that no one believes he killed Ron. Even Sam is convinced he's innocent. Don't let him throw his life away like this. I'll prove he didn't do this. I just need more time," Judy spoke with conviction.

18

Judy had been following David for hours. He made a few stops on his way home. He spent some time at his apartment on Bainbridge Island and then drove to a grocery store to shop. Judy watched him pick out fruit and some premade meals. She found it ironic that one of her mom's best cooks wouldn't cook for himself. He spent quite a bit of time looking at hair products before finally leaving the store. He seemed to be doing what anyone who hadn't had a day off in a while might do once given the time.

She started to wonder if her time would be better spent reviewing testimony with the occupants of Chase's apartment building. Judy decided that she would do just that if David went back to his apartment. She trailed him at a safe distance and almost lost him a time or two. Luckily, he didn't drive very fast. David turned his car in the direction of Poulsbo. He wasn't going home. Judy started to get a little anxious.

He drove along one of the curvy roads mentioned by the bike shop owner. After driving along the water for a short time, he moved inland through some of the Bainbridge Vineyard grape fields. The roads were no longer curvy, so Judy had to hang back to keep from being spotted. She watched as David's car moved off the paved road and started to leave a cloud of dust as it hurried up a gravel drive.

Judy pulled her Wrangler to the side of the road and climbed out quickly. She started to make her way through the grape vines to the building at the end of the drive. She wasn't sure what she would do if David came out of the building and started to drive away. She had no idea what she would say to Annie if she found her. Judy had confidence in her mother. If Lily believed Chase was innocent and that David was hiding something, she thought she was likely right on both counts. She had to investigate to the best of her ability and let the chips fall where they may.

As Judy cleared the grape vines and crossed the gravel driveway, she saw a small shack of a house. She crept up slowly, trying to stay low to avoid being spotted by anyone inside the small dwelling. Suddenly, she realized David or Annie could be the killer. Her mind started to race, "Maybe they did it together. If Annie was there that night, she and David may have gone to Ron's apartment after Chase left." Neither of them had an alibi that Judy knew of. "What kind of danger am I walking into?" As she talked to herself silently, she wondered if she should be here.

19

—·—

"**Y**our statement says you hit Ron in the head. What part of his head? Where on his person did you strike this life-ending blow?" Piper asked Chase.

Lily sat next to Piper facing Chase across a small table in a tiny well-lit room. Chase had a look of bewilderment on his face. "What do you mean? I hit him. I killed him. It's all right there in black and white. I want to plead guilty. I want you to enter this confession into evidence," he said sternly.

"You have to say specifically where you contacted his head," Piper went on.

"What did you hit him with?" Lily asked.

"I hit him with my fist. I closed my eyes when I swung but I'm pretty sure I hit him in the side of the face."

"What part of the face? Which side?" Piper asked as if she were cross-examining him on the witness stand.

"Listen. I'll write this up however you want me to. You're not going to badger me into changing my mind. Give it back. Tell me what else I need to add, and I'll add it. I did this, and I'm willing to pay the price for it. Let's get to it." Chase reached for the pad of paper in front of Piper. He scribbled a few sentences addressing the how and where of the impact.

"Let's talk about the timing of events," Piper said.

"No. Let's not," Chase said in an angry tone. "You work for me. I'm the client. I'm pleading guilty. I confess. There's nothing more for you to do here."

"There is so much more." Lily's eyes filled with tears.

"She's right. There's no death penalty in Washington state, so we don't have to worry about that, but you could spend the rest of your life behind bars. If we can show that it wasn't premeditated, that will help."

"Can we explain temporary insanity?" Lily pondered out loud. "Why did you hit him? You're always so kind and caring. You are always so even-tempered. What would cause you to do such a thing?"

"I never liked that guy. The mess in the kitchen was the last straw. I didn't mean to kill him. I swung at him and hit him. I left him for dead. I lied before. I hit him, and I killed him. I was the only one there. This is all on me. Do what you can, but I am willing to pay for my crime."

Lily reached for Chase's hand. He pulled it away, placing both of his hands in his lap under the table. Lily looked up at him with sorrowful, tear-filled eyes. She couldn't speak. She had no more words. Piper pushed her heavy chair back as she stood. She stepped to the door and called

Lily, "We need to go, Lily. Chase, I need you to re-write the statement so that it doesn't look amended. We will submit your statement when you finish."

Chase dropped his head and started to write. Lily sat staring at the top of his head for several minutes before she finally forced herself to leave him. The insulated door slammed loudly behind the two women. Within seconds, the door opened again, and Annie rushed through it ahead of Lily. "Don't," Annie begged through her tears. "Don't do this. I can't let you."

"What are you doing here? Annie, you have to leave. I'm responsible for Ron's death, and I am willing to go to prison for that," Chase insisted.

Judy and Piper joined Lily at the back of the room, closing the door. As they stood together in the cramped room, Annie turned away from Chase to look at the three women. "I did it. I hit Ron. He made a pass at me, and I closed my fist and gave him an uppercut to the jaw. I didn't think I hit him that hard. I didn't intend to kill him. I had no idea he was dead when I left. I hit him, and then, I ran. I called Chase. He said he would be home soon. He told me to leave right away. He told me to get away from Ron."

"You didn't kill him. I did," Chase said in a convincing manner. "He was fine when I got home. I started screaming at him the moment I entered the apartment. I hit him, and he died. I hit him in the jaw. I hit him harder than you did."

"The autopsy report did show a mild bruise to the jaw but that was superficial. Ron Castle died from trauma to the crown of his head. One of you may be telling the truth, but at least one of you is lying and we can't go to the DA with a half-baked story like this."

"Chase. You have to tell us the truth. We can help you if you tell us the truth," Lily begged.

"We are right back where we started," Judy said. "We told you at the beginning. We can only help you if you are honest with us.

"You told me an eyewitness saw Annie at my apartment that night," Chase said. "That makes her a suspect. Now, you know she fought with Ron. When all of this gets out, she will be the prime suspect. I'd rather take the blame. That's the truth. I want to carry on with the confession."

Piper stepped closer to Chase. "The DA has to prove that Annie did it. They must prove it beyond any reasonable doubt. They will be hard-pressed to do that on this shred of evidence. Without a confession, they would have trouble doing that in your case as well."

"We have been talking with all of your neighbors," Judy spoke up. "We have a very tight timeline of the events based on Woodrow Freeman's recollection of what TV shows he was watching at the time of events. Sam and Juice will testify that he was okay when they saw him. Everyone we talked to said that you would never do such a thing. The whole island will testify on your behalf as character witnesses. Let us continue to investigate. We'll figure this out."

"Don't confess. We will get through this. Both of us. Together," Annie pleaded with Chase.

Chase held the three-page confession in his hand, extending it to Piper. Are you sure about this? You really don't think they have a case against Annie?"

"They have very little." Piper looked directly into Chase's eyes.

He stood still for several minutes, studying Piper's face. He stared into her unblinking gaze and tore the papers in half. Annie took them from his hand and continued to tear them.

20

Judy and Lily drove to Bainbridge Island to visit the Castle residence. They hoped to get Ron Castle's parents to talk with them, but no one at the house answered the door. Judy also wanted to talk with the tenants in Chase's building one more time. She decided she'd start with whomever was home at the moment.

Lily knocked on doors 205 and 206 while Judy pounded on 201, 202, and 203 just seconds apart. Judy was hoping that talking to the neighbors together might bring some new information to light. Woody was the first resident of Building Two to answer his door. He opened the door wide, greeting Judy with a broad smile.

"Hi, Woody. How are you today?" Judy smiled warmly at Woody.

"Hi. You're Judy, right? I remember you. You're Chase's friend.

"Yes. That's right. Do you remember my mom, Lily?"

"Oh, yes. Hello, Lily. How are you today?"

Before Lily could respond to Woody's friendly greeting, the door across the hall opened and Valarie poked her head out.

"Hi, Valarie!" Woody's words erupted from his mouth. He seemed very happy to see his neighbor.

"Hi to everyone," Valarie said quizzically. "What's going on?"

"We wanted to talk with you and your neighbors again, about the night Ron Castle died. We are desperate to find some new information that will help Chase," Judy responded. "Did either of you remember anything about that morning that we haven't already discussed?"

"I saw Sam and Juice around two and then I went to bed. I don't think there's anything else for me to remember," Valarie said.

"Woody. You said you heard Chase yell Annie's name. Do you remember that?"

"I heard Chase yell her name. I sure did. I was trying to watch *The Twilight Zone*."

"Do you remember anything else he said? Mrs. Petrovsky heard him shouting at Ron, too." Judy was hopeful that Woody could help explain what Elenore Petrovsky had mentioned about "torching his grandma." She also hoped he had a different version of the comment about Chase threatening to kill Ron. She hadn't shared those comments with Chase at the prison. She didn't think that would help them talk Chase into declining to confess. At some point, they would need to ask him about what he screamed at Ron the night Ron died.

"I can't say I remember anything else he said. I remember him saying Annie's name. I like Annie. She's always nice to me. Sometimes she brings me pie. I like lemon meringue." Woody eagerly answered Judy's questions.

"Are you sure you didn't hear him say anything about his grandmother? Anything about a torch?"

"No. Just 'Annie.'" Woody nodded in confirmation of his statement.

"Is it possible that he said 'granny' and not 'Annie'?" Lily asked Woody.

"I don't think so." Woody squinted his eyes and scratched his head lightly. "I'm pretty sure he said 'Annie.'"

"What exactly did Mrs. Petrovsky say?" Valarie asked Judy.

"She said Chase yelled, 'Torch my grandma,'" Judy responded. She refrained from sharing the rest of what Elenore Petrovsky stated she heard.

"Is it possible she said 'granny' and not 'grandma'?" Lily asked.

Judy referred to her notes. "No. She said 'grandma.' I wrote it down exactly as she said it to me."

"Maybe that's how she translated it in her mind. Perhaps she misunderstood 'Annie' as 'Granny.' Lily offered.

"Would you ladies like to come in for some tea? I can put the kettle on," Woody offered with an inviting smile.

He seemed so eager for the company that Lily could not turn him down this time. "We would love some tea. May we come in?"

"Oh, yes. Please come in and have a seat at the table," he said as he moved to the stove.

Judy and Valarie grinned at each other and followed Lily into Woody's kitchen. The television was on as it was each time Judy had been to visit Woody.

"I have fresh lemons. Would anyone like sugar? It's so nice to have company for tea," Woody spoke quickly as he looked through his cupboards, pulling out cups as he spoke.

"Woody, do you recall hearing any commotion from next door the night Ron died? Was there any kind of struggle or the sound of someone hitting the ground? Anything like that?" Judy hoped he could verify there was no physical action at that time.

"No. Nothing like that. I turned up my TV. I was trying to listen to my show," he countered.

"Did you see or hear Annie that night?" Lily asked.

"Was Annie here?" Valarie questioned Lily.

"No, ma'am. I would remember if Annie was here. I like Annie. Sometimes, she brings me pie." Woody continued to work away at the counter.

Lily smiled at Valarie without answering her question. Instead, she redirected the conversation. "What are you watching today, Woody?"

"*Full House*. I love this show. Uncle Jesse is my favorite. He's played by John Stamos. He started out on *General Hospital,* you know. I like Elvis, too. Just like Jesse Katsopolis does. That's why I like him best. Do you like *Full House*?"

"I watched that all the time when I was a kid. I liked Stephanie Tanner. She was played by Jodie Sweetin," Judy joined in.

"I can't say I have ever watched the show," Valarie remarked.

"I always liked Danny. He was the voice of reason on the show. The other two guys were not very responsible," Lily said with a laugh.

"Bob Saget," Judy said abruptly. "We have to go. I'm sorry, Woody. I was looking forward to having tea with you, but there is something I must do. Come on, Lily!" Judy hurried to the door with Lily following close behind as Woody brought Valarie a cup of tea.

21

"Hello. Are you Dr. Weaver?" Judy asked the short, bright-eyed woman who came to the door.

"I'm Dr. Virginia Weaver. Who might you be, young lady?" She responded with a smile.

"I'm Judy Pine. This is my mom, Lily." Judy replied.

"It's a pleasure to meet you in person, Judy. I believe we've talked on the phone on several occasions. I imagine you're working on the Castle story," the doctor said.

"How did you know?" Lily asked with a bit of sarcasm.

"Not much else newsworthy going on around here at the moment," Virginia replied with a grin. "Come in. Have a seat."

Doctor Weaver ushered Judy and Lily into her office. It was small and cluttered but had a calmness about it. Judy and Lily immediately felt comfortable in the snug atmosphere. They took seats across from Virginia Weaver as she plopped into an oversized wooden chair with a handmade cushion on the seat.

"What can I do for you? I'm sure you've already read my report." Dr. Weaver leaned forward in anticipation of Judy's response.

"I did," Judy confirmed. Blunt force trauma to the top of the head. Crack in the skull. Some red fibers in the wound. Cranial bleeding. Your report said he died between two and five in the morning."

"Yes. That sounds correct. Do you have some reason to believe he didn't die at that time? Are you questioning my medical opinion on the matter?" Dr. Weaver's expression became a bit more serious.

"Oh, no. Not at all." Judy shook her head raising her eyebrows in apology. "I was hoping to ask you some medical questions in relation to the blow to the head that would have caused such an injury."

"From the wound on the top of Ron Castle's head, I'd say it had to have impacted something fairly large. It would have been quite an impact to make his skull crack like it did." Dr. Weaver studied the report as she spoke.

"You seem very sure about the time of death," Judy said.

"Yes. Due to the body temperature and rigor that had set in, I'm certain he died sometime between two and five. I wish I could be more specific," the doctor said with some regret. "I'm sure it would be helpful if I could. I'm sorry. Is this for your story?"

"Not exactly," Lily spoke up. "Chase Raker works for me. More than that. He's a close friend. We are trying to help him."

"Is Chase the boy who is accused of killing Ron?" Virginia asked.

"Yes. We'd like to prove he didn't do this. We're sure he's innocent." Lily let out a heavy sigh.

"You are sure he died between two and five, but are you sure his injury was inflicted between two and five?" Judy asked succinctly.

The friendly doctor squinted her eyes a bit and pursed her lips, trying to be sure she understood the direction Judy was leading her in.

"Could Ron have been assaulted earlier in the day without dying right away? How long could he have walked around with that head injury? Is it possible that the injury that killed him didn't happen immediately before his death?" Judy continued to rephrase, trying to make sure her question was clear.

"Well... yes. It's possible. Not highly likely, but possible. His skull was fractured. He had blood between his brain and his skull. The force from that would have likely made him feel nauseated and out of sorts if it hadn't killed him right away. He would likely have been suffering from quite a headache if he were walking around with that wound. People *have* been reported to have gone through a day or two with head trauma, later dying in their sleep. In those cases, there are usually witnesses to attest to the earlier trauma and to be with the victim just before their death." Dr. Weaver continued her gentle squint as if she were reading a medical journal article from deep within her memory.

"So, he may have been injured anytime within forty-eight hours of his death?" Lily questioned.

"I repeat. It's possible but not likely. There have been isolated cases. Usually closer to twenty-four hours from the time of the injury to death."

"Like Bob Saget," Lily said as if a light bulb went off in her head. She smiled at her daughter.

"Exactly," Judy remarked.

"Yes. Bob Saget died hours after a head injury. Ron's injury wasn't quite as massive a trauma from what I read about Mr. Saget, but it was surely enough to kill him."

"So, Ron's injury was less serious, meaning he would have been more likely to walk around for a while not realizing the extent of the injury." Judy sounded proud of her deduction. "Hopefully, this will help us broaden our suspect pool."

"Isn't a larger number of suspects a bad thing when you're trying to solve a murder?" the doctor asked.

"Usually, yes. But we are hoping to create as much reasonable doubt as possible," Judy responded with a wide smile that almost broke out into a laugh.

"I'm happy to note in the final report that Ron Castle died from a wound that could have *possibly* occurred up to twenty-four or forty-eight hours before his death." The doctor shrugged her shoulders.

"That's all we are asking. Thank you! Thank you very much!" Judy shook the doctor's hand jubilantly and turned for the door.

"Yes. We are very grateful for your help, Dr. Weaver." Lily smiled at the doctor and shook her hand slowly with a soft caring grip.

22

Judy checked her appearance in the hall mirror before answering the door. Jack yipped at the threshold, warning Judy of the intruder. Judy was confident that she was about to greet Peter Crum at the door. Peter and Judy had met during a case involving a hit and run several months ago. Peter worked as a detective in the Tacoma area. She had contacted him regarding some leads on stories that she was working on in his jurisdiction. Truth be told, she contacted him more in the interest of getting to know him better. After months of casual investigatory conversations, Peter finally asked her out on a date.

For their first date, Peter escorted Judy to a fine dining establishment in downtown Tacoma. The kind of place where the prices aren't on the menu. The lighting was romantic, and a pianist played a grand piano in the middle of the dining room. The food was perfect, and the evening was full of friendly banter and laughter.

Judy considered this their second official date. She had offered to make dinner for Detective Crum. He was a few minutes early but that was expected. He was always a little overly punctual. Judy didn't mind. She was excited to see him again. She smiled brightly as she opened the door.

"Thank you for agreeing to eat in tonight. I've been leaving Jack with Wendy more than usual. I wanted to stay with him this evening." Judy walked to the kitchen as Peter stepped inside, kneeling next to Jack. Jack leaned his front paws on Peter's leg as Peter scratched Jack's chin. Peter lifted Jack to his chest with one hand and followed Judy to the kitchen.

"I love a home-cooked meal," Peter said as he took a stool at the kitchen island. He continued to hold Jack cradled in his arm. "He's a friendly little guy." Jack seemed to be smiling as he stretched his small chin towards Peter for more scratching.

"He'll let you hold him all night. Especially if you keep scratching him like that. He loves to have his ears rubbed too," she said with a slight chuckle.

Judy melted a few ounces of butter in a large skillet and added heavy cream. There were three more pots sitting on the stovetop.

"That looks like quite a feast you're working on there," Peter said.

"It's just Alfredo. I have fettucine boiling along with some broccoli and sautéed mushrooms. There's chicken in the oven along with some artesian bread. Don't be too impressed. The chicken is rotisserie chicken I bought pre-cooked from the store."

"Artesian bread sounds impressive."

"I bought that already made too. I'm just warming it up," she confessed with a smile.

"Sounds delightful. How's the case going? The murder case with the guy who works for your mom?"

"We hope to establish the fact that he may have been struck the day before he died. If we can, at least convince the DA that there was a longer window of time for the murder, we may be able to get Chase out until the prosecutor builds a stronger case. He's not coping very well in jail, but he was willing to stay in there for life if it meant saving his girlfriend. Chivalry is not dead."

"I'm glad you were able to talk him out of signing a confession. It's hard to turn back from that once it's done. He would have had to make a plea deal at that point, which surely would have included decades of jail time."

"He and Annie are a very sweet couple. I hate to see them going through all of this. We are meeting Sam and Juice tomorrow to talk with them about where Ron was and what he was doing the day before his death. We have an entirely new gap of time to account for. If we can prove that Ron had an altercation with someone other than Chase, it will help with his case."

"Even though Bainbridge Island isn't part of my territory, I'm happy to help in any way I can. Let me know if there's anything I can do."

"Oh. You know I will. Have you found me to be bashful so far?"

"Not a bit. I was expecting you to ask me out before I was confident enough to do it myself," he smiled with his eyes as he spoke.

"I thought it was obvious that I wanted you to ask me out. I was starting to wonder what kind of a detective you were. I dropped plenty of clues." Judy laughed as she brought the food to the island. She had a bowl of steaming fettuccine alongside a creamy Alfredo sauce. Sliced chicken, sauteed mushrooms, and steamed broccoli were all placed in separate dishes in the middle of the table. "It's build your own pasta." Judy smiled at Peter. She poured a bowl of food for Jack, and Peter lowered him gently to the floor.

23

S am and Juice were waiting in the yard in front of
Juice's house when Lily and Judy pulled up.

"Hi, Mrs. Pine and Miss Pine," Juice smiled as he started
the conversation.

"Judy," Judy quickly offered.

"Please call me Lily. How are you two today? I'm very
sorry about your brother, Sam."

"Thanks, Lily. I'm sorry that my dad wouldn't speak to
you at our house. He's a very private man. He won't talk
to anyone except the police," Sam said.

"I understand," Judy said as she stepped closer to the
two young men. They stood in the grass near a large maple
tree, just out of the tree's shade. "It's such a nice day."

"Yes," Juice agreed. "If it's okay with you two, I'd prefer
to talk out here. I'd invite you in, but my mom isn't feeling
well."

"This is fine. We appreciate you talking with us today,"
Judy said. "We were hoping to get more information about

Ron's day. The day *before* he died. Friday. You told me Ron had the day off. Isn't that correct?"

"We all did," Sam responded. "We had lunch together and went for a bike ride."

"Sam and I went to the casino for poker and dinner. Ron didn't want to go," Juice added.

"Do you have any idea what Ron did before you met him for lunch?" Judy asked.

"Sleeping. He was still asleep when we got to his place." Sam sighed as he spoke of his brother. "He crawled off the couch, put on a hat, and we left. We ate at The Hideout. They have great burgers."

"There's one with peanut butter, bacon, and bananas," Juice added with a grin.

"Peanut butter on a burger? That sounds terrible." Judy made a sour face at the thought.

"I think it sounds like a terrific idea." Lily made a mental note of the concoction.

"So, you saw Ron get up for the day. The three of you ate burgers at a place called The Hideout. After that, you went for a bike ride?" Judy was clarifying.

"We had our bikes in the truck. We tossed Ron's in while we were at his place," Juice said. "We went on a quick ride. Sam and I wanted to go to The Point. Ron didn't want to go. He asked us to take him home. We didn't see him again until about one in the morning. We played video games for a short while and went home."

"Did anything odd happen during lunch or on the ride? Anything unusual about Ron during the drive?" Judy was taking notes in her usual pad.

"Nothing seemed out of the ordinary to me except that he didn't want to go to the casino for hold'em."

"What's that?" Lily asked.

"It's a poker game. We go to The Point Casino a couple of times a month to play," Sam responded. "Ron won quite a bit the last time we went. He was so stoked." A glimmer of joy came to Sam's eyes as he talked about how happy his brother was.

"But he didn't go with you the day before he died?" Judy confirmed.

"No. he wanted to go home." The smile left Sam's eyes.

"Where did you ride?" Lily asked.

"Heritage Park in Port Gamble," Juice said, noticing Sam was getting a little choked up. "There are a bunch of trails there. Ron was full of energy when we got out of the truck. He took off ahead of us pretty quickly. As usual. He was flying around like he owned the place."

"Were there many other riders on the trail? Anyone Ron may have encountered?" Judy asked.

"No," Juice continued. We didn't see very many people out that day." He looked at Sam for confirmation. After receiving a head nod from his friend, he went on. "I didn't see much of Ron until we got off Iceman Trail. We skipped over to Jump to Conclusions and found Ron at the bottom."

"That's when he said he was ready to go home," Sam finished Juice's thought.

"Was that strange at all?" Judy asked. "Was it out of the ordinary for him to ask to go home at that point in the ride?"

Juice started to laugh. "Ron rode hard and fast. He didn't care where anyone else was. He was out to ride his heart out. At any point in a ride, he'd decide he'd had enough and want to call it quits. I think he would ride himself into exhaustion."

"Is it a hard trail?" Lily asked.

"Not for us," Sam stated firmly. "We ride that trail all the time. We know it as well as anyone. We had a good ride, and we went back home. No one bothered us."

"Did you talk to anyone at the park? Did Ron talk to anyone there?" Judy asked.

"No. I don't think we did," Sam said.

"There was one guy I noticed," Juice said. "He was walking his bike near Ron when we came off the last hill at Jump to Conclusions, but I don't know that they talked. I only remember it because we've ridden with the guy. He goes on the bike shop rides sometimes. I think his name is Monte."

"Do you think Monte may have had a disagreement with Ron? Did Ron say anything about him? Did he seem upset when you met up with him?" Judy rattled off questions.

"No. He didn't say much at all. He seemed perfectly calm to me. He just asked to go home." Sam had tears forming in his sad, brown eyes. Juice nodded in agreement.

"Burgers, biking, and then you two went to play poker. Is that about it?" Judy scribbled in her pad, sighing softly.

"Chase didn't do this... right?" Sam stuttered a bit as he spoke. "I can't believe Chase killed my brother."

"We don't believe that either, Sam." Lily put her hand on Sam's shoulder "We are sorry about your brother, and we are determined to prove Chase didn't kill him. We hope to figure out who the real killer is."

"What about the night before the burgers and the bike ride?" Judy continued the interview. "Do you know what Ron was doing the night before?"

"I called him around eight that night to see if he wanted to go to The Hideout for lunch with us," Sam offered. "He said he was watching old *Mash* episodes. He had run into Woody in the hallway, and Woody told him *Mash* was on TV Land. He liked *Mash*, but he didn't want to watch it with Woody because Woody would talk through the whole thing." Sam chucked a bit through his tears. "He said he had been watching TV since he got home from work and was planning to stay up until they stopped showing episodes of *Mash*. The TV was still on when we woke him for lunch. I assumed he had fallen asleep before TV Land changed to another series."

"That sounds uneventful," Lily grinned at her daughter.

"Anything else we can do to help?" Juice asked.

"I don't think so," Judy responded. "Thank you both for talking with me again."

24

"Should we stop and see Woody? Maybe he can tell us if anything happened at the apartment the day before Ron died. He talked to Ron even if no one else did," Judy said as she pulled her Wrangler away from the curb in front of Juice's small home.

"Maybe we need to talk to everyone at the apartment complex again. The doc said twenty-four to forty-eight hours before he died. It sounds like he worked and then watched TV and slept up to the time Sam and Juice have accounted for. The people in his building would have been the most likely to have encountered him. Sam and Juice were with him except for the time they spent at the casino. When I talked to Sam the other night, he told me Ron had spent the evening on the sofa in front of the TV before they all played video games at one in the morning."

"We should check in with Ron's employer. Maybe something happened at work. He was at work within the forty-eight-hour window. It's not likely that he was assaulted that long before his death, but according to the doctor, it's slightly possible."

Soon the two women found themselves back in the hall of Ron and Chase's apartment building, knocking on all of the doors.

"This is getting to be a bit of a bad habit," Judy laughed.

Woody was the first one to answer his door. "Judy, Lily, it's so nice to see you. I'm sorry you couldn't stay for tea when you were here last time."

Judy was surprised that Woody seemed to have such a keen recollection of their last visit. "Sorry, something suddenly came up."

Woody started to laugh. 'I was just watching *The Brady Bunch* episode where Marsha asks Greg how to get out of a date with one guy to go out with another guy. Greg told her to say, 'Something suddenly came up.'"

"I remember that one," Lily said with a short laugh.

"We came by to ask if you remember seeing Ron two nights before he died. Sam said he mentioned talking to you," Lily said. "Ron told Sam that you let him know *Mash* was on."

"Oh, yes. I remember. I asked him to come in and watch *Mash* with me. I know how much he loves Mash. He said he was tired. He didn't come in." Woody looked sad as he spoke.

"Was that it? Did he talk to you about anything else?" Judy asked.

"Not to me. He talked to her." He pointed down the hall where Valarie was entering the building.

"201 right?" Judy said to Valarie Marshal as she approached them.

"Yes. Please. Call me 201," Valarie said with a laugh. "I've been called worse things."

"Sorry. I just wanted to be sure I had the vantage point correct in my mind. Did you talk to Ron last Thursday?" Judy went on with her investigation after a slight apology.

"You remember. I was telling Ron about *Mash* being on. I asked if you and Ron wanted to come in and watch it with me." Woody was very eager to tell the story.

"I remember. You were going on about television, and Ron was mumbling softly. Something about a bike. He didn't make much sense... wait... That wasn't Thursday. It was Friday. It was the day Ron died. Well, the day before. It was around dinner time. Ron had just gotten his pizza from the delivery guy. Woody, you were talking about *The Twilight Zone* marathon starting at midnight, not *Mash*."

Woody cocked his head and thought for a minute. The ladies all stood patiently waiting for him to speak. He squinted his eyes a little and said, "Yes. You were in the hall Friday. Not Thursday. Now, I remember. I came out when I heard the pizza guy knock."

"When I walked up, the delivery guy was leaving, and you were telling Ron how excited you were about *The Twilight Zone* marathon that was starting later.

Ron mumbled incoherently and went back inside. I think he said something about a bike. Woody smiled and I shrugged, and we all ducked into our respective dwellings."

"What do you mean by 'mumbled,' dear?" Lily asked."

"Most of what he said was hard to understand. He spoke softly, but it wasn't that I couldn't hear him. His words just didn't make any sense." Valarie looked at Woody for support as she spoke.

Woody shrugged but didn't offer more.

"Are you sure that that happened the day he died?"

"Yes. It was earlier in the day on Friday. I think it must have been around dinner time. I was just getting home with some groceries. I had picked up some sauce and noodles to make pasta."

"Do you know anything about his bike? He went mountain biking with Sam and Juice earlier that day. Could you make out anything else he said? Anything at all?"

"No. I just got the one word. Did you understand any of it Woody?" Valarie turned to her tall, sweet neighbor.

"I just don't remember. I know there was pizza one night. *Mash* was on another night." Woody tapped the fingers on his left hand one at a time with the index finger of his right hand. He seemed to be trying to calculate in his mind. After a few minutes, he shook his head and said, "No."

25

"Piper, we need to see Ron's bike. His mountain bike. Can we get access to it?" Judy asked as she sipped her coffee on the coffee shop patio. Her little Yorkie sat in her lap.

"We should be able to. Is this related to what you told me yesterday about the change in the medical examiner's report?" Piper pulled her sweater closed as the wind blew in her face.

"I'm sorry. Are you cold? We can go inside if you prefer. I think they'll be okay with Jack in there. I'm sure I've seen dogs inside the coffee shop before."

"That's okay. I'm fine. Tell me about the two-day window."

"Do you remember Bob Saget?"

"The dad on *Full House*?"

"Yes. He died of a subdural hematoma the day after a trauma to his head. Dr. Weaver said it's possible that Ron suffered a similar injury. His injury wasn't as severe as Bob Saget's, but he could have been assaulted the day before he died. Due to the crack in his skull, he had a blood pool between his skull and his brain. It appears to have been formed over time. She can't be sure how much time. She also can't be sure when the injury occurred. She just said it is possible that it occurred the day before. There is a slight chance it happened as much as forty-eight hours before it killed him."

"I get that... and it's great news. Well, great for Chase. This means he may not have been killed in the two to five in the morning window just after Chase was heard threatening Ron. I don't understand what this has to do with his mountain bike."

"I'm not sure I do either. Valarie Marshal said Ron mumbled something about a bike on Friday night when the pizza guy came."

"I don't understand what a bike and a pizza have to do with the investigation."

"The day before Ron died, he went to lunch and for a bike ride with Sam and Juice. That night, he stayed at his house watching TV. He ordered a pizza but didn't eat it. He mumbled something about a bike to Valarie. I need to find out if someone hit Ron over the head during that time. I want to figure out why he would have been mumbling about a bike."

"Okay. I'll get you into the apartment to check for the bike. What about the brother and his friend?"

"Juice and Sam? They were with him from the time he woke up on Friday until they dropped him off at home before they went to The Point Casino to play cards. As you know, they played video games with him early the next morning."

"So, you think someone may have hit Ron while he was at home before Sam and Juice came back from their card game?"

"Something like that. I have one more lead to track down while you get me through the red tape to see the bike."

"Be careful. It's my experience that when you get close to discovering a killer, you put yourself in danger."

"I'll be careful. I'm just going to play a little card game of my own. I call it three-card Monte."

26

Annie and Judy waited in the visiting room full of inmates and their discussions with friends and family. The murmur was loud and distracting to Judy. She was sure there was a room full of newspaper stories here. Her attention shifted as Chase was brought into the room. He sat down next to Annie, and she started to cry.

"We are going to get him out of here," Judy told Annie, with a promising tone. "I need to understand some things that happened. Some things that were said. I believe you are the only ones who can explain."

"Anything. I'll tell you anything you want to know. I'll do whatever it takes to get Chase out of jail." Tears ran down Annie's smooth cheeks as she looked into Chase's eyes.

"I'll be okay. Don't worry about me," Chase tried to sound relaxed. He wanted to bring some comfort to Annie. "Tell us what you need to know."

"This is going to sound bad, but I'm sure you can shed some light on it," Judy said. "Elenore Petrovsky said she heard you say 'I'll kill you' before she called the police.

Annie's emotions erupted in a rush of tears. Her body shook as she leaned forward and put her head on the table.

"I did say that," Chase admitted, "Ron grabbed Annie. He was inappropriate. He tried to kiss her. She called me while I was on the ferry. She told me about it before I could get home. I was drunk and mad."

"Is that what happened, Annie?" Judy looked at her, waiting for Annie to regain some composure and speak to her.

Annie lifted her head and wiped her eyes. "I went to Chase's apartment to wait for him. I knocked on the door, but there was no answer. I have a key, so I let myself in. Ron was on the couch watching television. He got up when I walked in. He seemed a little unstable as he stood. I think he was drunk. I told him I wouldn't disturb him while he watched his movie. I was just waiting for Chase to get home. He stumbled over to me and grabbed me by the neck. He pulled me towards him and tried to kiss me." She wiped her nose as tears continued to cover her face.

"Is that when you hit him?" Judy asked.

"Yes. I pushed myself away from him and curled my knuckles and pulled back my arm. He started to come closer again, and I let him have it. As he was stumbling backward, I ran out of the apartment. I called Chase once I got to my car."

"Why were you hiding? What were you doing in that shack in the vineyard?" Judy continued her questioning.

"When Lily told me Ron was dead, I thought I must have killed him. Since Chase was in jail, I called David. He took me there. He told me not to talk to anyone until we figured out what to do. I wanted to see Chase." She looked up at him. "I wanted to come to you."

"I know. I love you. I know you wanted to help. David was trying to help you." Chase reached for Annie's hand. He looked at the guard nearest them as he took her hand in his. The guard didn't react, so he held her hand and tried to smile.

"I love you too. I want to get you out of this awful place," Annie responded.

"You were hiding because you thought you might be responsible. Chase wanted to confess to save you from going to prison. Mrs. Petrovsky thought you wanted Ron to torch your grandma." Judy said.

"I'm sorry. Mrs. Petrovsky said what?" Chase had a baffled look on his face.

"She said she heard you say, 'Torch my grandma' and 'I'll kill you.'" Judy replied.

"I said, 'If you *touch* my *Annie* again, I'll kill you.'"

"Granny. Annie. Lily was right." Judy said softly to herself.

Judy stood and smiled at the couple. "One more thing. Do you know of anything red and fibrous that may have been used to strike Ron? Anything in the apartment? It would have to be something fairly large and hard to cause such an injury.

They both shook their heads as Judy stood and stewed on her thoughts for a moment.

27

"I imagine that you are all wondering why I asked you here," Judy said as she looked around the dining room of Marty's on the Bay. Sam, Juice, Monte, David, and Annie sat with Lily at a round table near the bar. Dr. Weaver, the district attorney, and Piper were at a small table next to them.

Judy paced in front of the two tables talking loudly as if she were making her closing argument in a murder trial. "Sadly, Ron Castle died sometime between two and five last Saturday morning. According to the county medical examiner, Dr. Virginia Weaver," Judy paused and nodded at Dr. Weaver. The rest of the group turned to look at her. "Chase suffered a subdural hematoma. He had a crack in his skull that let blood pool in his skull. He could have walked around with this injury for as long as a day or two. Is that correct, Dr. Weaver?'

"Yes," Dr. Weaver confirmed with a nod. "It's much likelier that it happened within twenty-four hours of his death."

"That means Ron sustained the injury sometime between Thursday afternoon and Saturday at five in the morning."

Ron went home from work Thursday and watched television until he fell asleep on the couch. He talked to Woody about *Mash* on his way in. As far as we know, he didn't leave his apartment on Thursday night through Friday morning, and no one was with him during that time. Woody saw him around six pm on Thursday. Sam and Juice woke him up close to noon on Friday. I couldn't find a single witness who saw anyone come or go from the apartment during that time."

"That's right," Woody said with a huge grin. "I saw him. We talked about *Mash*. I asked him to come watch with me, but he said no. He went into his apartment. I watched it anyway. It was on all night."

Judy went on. "Sam and Juice found Ron sleeping on the sofa the next day around noon and took him out for a burger. They proceeded to Port Gamble to ride trails at Heritage Park." Judy was reading from her small notepad. "Ron rode off in front of them, but they caught up to him at the bottom of the Jump to Conclusions trail where they saw you with him, Monte Quinn." She pointed at Monte as she said his name.

"Yes," Monte spoke from his seat. "Like I told you, I saw him take a spill. The dude wasn't even wearing a helmet. He lost it on the last hill and went over the handlebars. I stopped to check on him. He said he was fine and told me to get lost."

"Juice, you said he wanted to go home when you found him at the bottom of the trail." Judy went back into her summation.

Juice nodded his agreement but looked confused.

"Sam, you told us he was quiet on the way home and didn't talk much later that night when you played video games. Is that right?" Judy stopped pacing in front of Sam.

"He was quieter than usual. I didn't think much of it. He didn't tell us he wrecked his bike."

"He was hard to understand but mumbling about his bike when I saw him Friday night before dinner," Valarie Marshal spoke up.

Judy began again. "Ron ordered a pizza around six but..."

Juice interrupted her. "He hadn't eaten any of it. The pizza was whole when I asked if I could have a slice. There wasn't a single piece taken out of it."

"He went over his handlebars, likely hitting his head on the ground, a tree, or possibly a rock. I checked his bike. It had damage but was still rideable. He was quiet and sometimes incoherent. He didn't have an appetite. He was wearing a Georgia Bulldogs hat while riding. He was not wearing a cap when officers found him Saturday morning. What do you make of all this, Dr. Weaver?" Judy sat abruptly in a chair next to Dr. Weaver and tilted her head in the doctor's direction as if she was turning the audience over to her.

"Ron Castle's injury could have been caused by hitting a tree or a log after going over the handlebars of a bike at a high speed. A subdural hematoma can cause confusion, headaches, and loss of appetite."

"So, he could have died from a bike injury that happened more than twelve hours before his death?" Sam asked.

"Yes. It's entirely possible," the doctor responded. "There were some red fibers found in the wound that could have come from a Georgia ball cap. We would have to run some tests on the cap."

"If this is true, we might have been able to save him if he would have told us about the injury. If he had only told us. If he didn't have such a big ego. If he could have admitted he wrecked his bike..." Sam trailed off.

"He probably didn't think it was that serious," the doctor tried to comfort Sam. "Many times, people suffer head injuries that they think are minor only to experience major complications later."

"A helmet might have helped," Juice said softly.

Piper approached Judy and Lily after walking the district attorney to the door. "The DA has agreed to release Chase while they continue the investigation. He never had much evidence against Chase to start with. After hearing your story, he agrees that it could very well have been an accident. He will send a forensics team to the park. He will also contact a neurological specialist to confirm Dr. Weaver's interpretation of the injuries. In the meantime, Chase will be released from jail."

Killer Christmas in Paradise

A Pacific Northwest Cozy Culinary Mystery – Book 4

Sample Chapter

Chapter 1

"It's beautiful up here. I'm so glad you talked me into coming," Lily said as she trudged through the snow in her cumbersome snowshoes.

"Yes, this is breathtaking," Jed agreed.

"I told you both it would be worth the effort and endurance of the cold temperatures." Judy looked back at Jed and her mother, pausing her incline for the moment.

Judy, Lily, and Jed had started climbing the Sky Line trail near Paradise, Washington hours ago. The views of Mount Rainier were breathtaking. The sun had been shining brightly most of the day, reflecting radiantly off the snow-covered ground. The three hikers removed their sunglasses as dark, menacing clouds threatened to capture the open sky.

"Maybe we should hurry along back to the car. It looks like we are close to finishing the trail loop." Jed looked up at the sky.

"The weather forecast wasn't calling for snow, but I agree with Jed. Let's get a little boogie in our steps. I don't want to get caught out here in a snowstorm." Judy hurried her pace as much as she could as she led the way.

Snow started to fall quickly in large flakes as Lily stepped out of her snowshoes and climbed into the passenger seat of Judy's four-door Wrangler. Jed took both of their snowshoes to the back of the Jeep. "We better put the chains on," Jed suggested as he opened the back of the jacked-up SUV.

"I guess this is why we are required to carry chains up here," Judy said with a smirk. "I know I complained about being forced to have them, but it looks like those chains might be useful after all."

"Do you need my help?" Lily offered from the front seat.

"No," Jed responded quickly. "You stay put. I'll get the chains laid out. Go ahead, get the Jeep started, and turn on the heat." He smiled at Judy.

"Glad to," Judy responded. "I'm getting cold again now that we are standing still. Let me know when you are ready."

"Once he had the chains in place and the chain keepers attached, Jed instructed Judy to slowly drive forward until he signaled her to stop. He tightened the chains on all four tires and moved into the back seat of the Wrangler.

"Put her in low four and drive out of the lot. After a few hundred yards, let's stop and check the chains to make sure they are tight," Jed instructed Judy.

Judy put the Jeep in four-wheel drive and moved forward at about fifteen miles an hour until Jed told her to stop. The snow was now falling heavily and starting to blow sideways as Jed exited the vehicle to inspect the chains. While he checked the tires, Judy got out of the SUV and fought the heavy wind to reenter the Wrangler in the back seat.

"You don't want to drive?" Jed chuckled nervously as he got in behind the wheel. He rubbed his gloved hands together and leaned his face into the heat that blew from the air vent in the dash.

"Usually, yes. I like to be in control, but it drives quite a bit differently with the chains on. I thought someone with more experience driving with chains in the snow would give us a better chance of not ending up being pedestrians out here," Judy responded.

"I sure don't want to end up walking again. This snowstorm is getting out of hand. I thought you said there was no snow in the forecast." Lily raised her eyebrows at Judy as she turned to look at her from the front passenger seat.

"Storms are known to come up out of nowhere around here. The weathermen don't always see them coming. It's getting hard to see. We need to find a place to take shelter before this becomes a complete whiteout." Jed held the steering wheel tightly in his hands. He could feel his fingers getting sore from the nervous grip. He leaned into the flat front windshield, trying to see as far ahead as he could. He was only able to see about ten feet in front of the vehicle, and his line of sight was getting worse as they drove.

"We shouldn't be too far from the Paradise Inn," Judy said confidently. "It's not open this time of year, but I think the Jackson Memorial Visitor Center there is open all year long."

"The visitors center is only open on the weekends in the winter. They close down during the week since there isn't much action this time of year. Since this is Wednesday and Christmas is this Friday, they might be closed for the next week. Maybe two, with New Year's Day coming," Jed said.

"I should try to text Wendy. She is expecting us to pick up the dogs tonight.

Luckily, my restaurant is closed tomorrow and Wednesday for Christmas Eve and Christmas Day. I like the staff to be off for the holiday. If we get stuck up here, at least it won't affect business," Lily sighed.

"That means no one will miss us," Judy interjected.

"Surely your new love interest, Peter, will miss you," Lily said with a sly grin.

"I'm not sure that will be the case. We had a bit of a tiff yesterday. I'm afraid he may not be expecting to see me for a few days." Judy shifted her puckered lips side to side as she stewed on her words.

"Quit talking like that. We don't need to worry about being trapped in a snowstorm. We will get to the Inn and hold up until the storm passes. We may have to break in, but we can leave a note and pay for any damages later. I'm sure they will understand." Jed kept his eyes glued to the windshield as the chained tires crept closer to the Paradise Inn.

"My text isn't going through," Lily said with a sigh. "No cell reception."

"We should be getting close, but I can't see anything. Are you sure you're still on the road, Jed?" Judy leaned forward between the front bucket seats, peering at the whiteout through the front windshield.

"No. I'm not sure," Jed said. "I'm using the compass to keep heading in the general direction of the inn, but I can't see the edge of the road anymore. I can't tell where we are for sure. Do you think we should pull over and try to wait it out in the car until the visibility improves?"

Before either of the women could respond, the Jeep Wrangler started to slide sideways, coming to an abrupt stop in the snow.

"Yes. I think we should stop," Judy said with a laugh.

"Is everyone okay?" Jed asked as he turned his head from the windshield for the first time since they got into the SUV.

"I'm okay," Lily confirmed.

"Me too," Judy added. "What should we do now? Can you back up? Do you think you can get back on the road?"

Jed firmly grabbed the gear shift and put the transmission into reverse. The Jeep growled and one of the tires seemed to spin, but the SUV stayed in the same position in the snowbank. Jed moved the gear shift into drive and then back to reverse several times. It was no use. The Jeep wasn't going anywhere. The question was, were the passengers?

Lily looked out her side window to see nothing but white. "We aren't getting out on this side. Are you two able to open the driver's side doors?"

"We have a half tank of gas. Maybe we should sit in here with the heat running as long as we can. The snow might let up. Maybe someone will come along and find us." Judy suggested.

"I'm sorry. It looks like I got off the road, and we slid into a ravine. I should have stopped sooner. I wanted to try to get to the inn without having to make you get out and walk. I'm not sure how long it will take to walk to shelter in this wind and snow. I think we should get moving. I don't want to end up walking in the dark. I vote we get our snowshoes on and get layered up for a walk."

"I guess being out here in the dark would suck." Judy pulled her phone from her parka and checked for a signal.

"Do you expect to get cell service here?" Lily asked.

"I read that a cell tower was installed in the attic of the Jackson Memorial Visitor Center. I thought we might be close enough to pick up a signal, but so far, I don't have service." Judy responded.

"She's right," Jed confirmed. "Some limited-service equipment was installed in the attic. I think we'll need to get pretty close to get access, but we could call for help if we can make it to the visitor center. We can hold up there or in the Paradise Inn. They're fairly close together. Stay here. I'll check to see if I can open the back door."

Jed pushed his door open and climbed into the snow as the wind whirled into the cab of the Jeep. He yanked at the back door handle. The door opened about three-fourths of the way before being stopped by the snowbank. He was able to open the glass most of the way. "Lean one of the seats down and climb back here, Judy. Once you get your snowshoes on, you can hop out, and Lily can do the same."

Jed pulled his snowshoes out into the snow as Judy climbed into the back of the Wrangler. Judy put her shoes on and then helped her mother. They stepped back from the Jeep and slammed the door.

"Not that it matters very much, but do you have the keys?" Judy asked as she leaned around the side of the Jeep to where she expected to see Jed on the road. "Where is he? Where's Jed?"

Lily stepped onto the snow-covered roadway and grabbed Judy's arm. "I don't know. I don't see him anywhere."

"Jed!" Lily and Judy screamed repeatedly. Their words seemed to get lost in the wind and snow.

"I can barely see the glove in front of my face," Judy said.

"What do you think happened to him? What direction do we go? How are we going to find him? How will we get to shelter?"

Recipes

Build Your Own Alfredo for 2

1 pound chicken breast

2 tablespoons avocado oil

2 teaspoons of Italian seasoning

1 pint sliced mushrooms

2 tablespoons butter

8 ounces of broccoli florets

1 teaspoon of salt

1 teaspoon of freshly ground pepper

4 ounces of fettuccini noodles

Take-and-bake hearty-grain bread

Alfredo sauce

2 tablespoons butter

1 pint of heavy whipping cream

10 ounces of freshly grated parmesan cheese

- Mix avocado oil, ½ teaspoon each of salt, pepper, and Italian seasoning in a medium-sized bowl.

- Add chicken breast and coat with oil mixture.

- Grill chicken breast to an internal temperature of 165 degrees.

- While chicken grills, place a large pot of water on a burner on high heat to boil.

- Bake bread per directions on the label.

- Once the water starts to boil, add fettuccine noodles, and turn the heat to medium-high.

- Boil pasta per box instructions.

- Place a small skillet on a burner on medium heat.

- Add two ounces of butter and the mushrooms to the skillet.

- Stir occasionally until mushrooms are heated through and slightly browned around the edges.

- Place a small pot half full of water on a burner on high heat.

- Once water is boiling, add ½ teaspoon of salt and the broccoli florets.

- Cover pot and steam broccoli for 5-8 minutes to your liking.

- Start sauce by adding 2 tablespoons of butter to a large nonstick skillet at medium heat.

- Once the butter melts, add the heavy cream. Stir occasionally until it starts to bubble.

- Add parmesan cheese in 4 parts, stirring until the cheese melts each time.

- Add more parmesan or use less cream for a thicker sauce.

- Once the chicken is cooked to an internal temperature of 165 degrees, remove from grill.

- Let the chicken rest while you drain the broccoli and pasta.

- Slice chicken into ½ inch strips.

- Turn all burners off.

- I like to serve the mushrooms and sauce right from the stovetop and the noodles and broccoli from the colanders.

- Slice the bread and hand out the plates.

***

3rd Wheel Peanut Butter and Banana Burger

1 pound of ground beef – 20% fat

Salt, to taste

Pepper, to taste

1 tablespoon butter

3 tablespoons of creamy peanut butter

One banana – ripe

9 slices of center-cut bacon

- Divide the ground beef into 3 equal portions and gently form into approximately ½-inch thick patties that are wider than the bun you are using.

Sprinkle salt and pepper on both sides and grill to the preferred temperature.

- Butter buns with equal parts of butter and grill until lightly toasted.

- Fry bacon to the desired doneness.

- Slice banana into ¼ inch slices.

- Warm peanut butter in the microwave for 20-30 seconds until runny.

- Smear equal parts of the peanut butter on each bun top and add slices of banana to cover the bun top.

- When burgers are cooked to your desired temperature, remove from the grill and let them rest for five minutes.

- Place burgers on the bottom bun and cover each burger with three slices of bacon.

- Place bun tops, with peanut butter and bananas on top, of bacon burgers.

— ◆ —

Please visit **dshock.net** for more books by Dennis Shock.

Made in the USA
Las Vegas, NV
08 January 2024

84050048R00079